THE LAST NOEL

A SLEIGHVILLE NOVEL
BOOK 3

AMANDA SIEGRIST

McCord Family Novel

Protecting You

Trust in Love

Deserving You

Always Kind of Love

Finding You

Dare You to Love

Mona & Mason

The Paranormal Chronicles, Volume I

Perfect For You Novel

The Wrong Brother

The Right Time

The Easy Part

The Hard Choice

Psychic Love Novel

Exploding Love

Captured Love

Slaying Love Novel

Won't Let You Go

Doomed Love

Deadly Crazy

Evidence of Sin

Finding Redemption

Obsessed Hope

Short Stories

Paint By Murder

Follow Me, Sweet Darling

Sleighville Novel

Dashing Through the Fear

Here Comes Chaos

The Last Noel

Standalone Novel

The Danger with Love

Conquering Fear Novel

Co-written with Jane Blythe

Drowning in You

Out of the Darkness

Closing In

1

——————

He stared at the woman, mesmerized for a moment at the destruction that glared back. Then Duke shook his head, tearing his gaze away from the photo hanging on the board.

Such a young life to have been taken away too soon. The only question he wanted to answer was who had taken it.

They'd pulled Beth Terden's body out of the lake over five months ago, back in May. Oddly enough, about a year from the day she had left town. Or so they thought. She hadn't left at all. Her life had been snuffed out, taken away from her.

Griffin had handed him the reins to the case. And what had he uncovered so far?

Jack shit!

She'd been a loner in town. When he interviewed people, going shop to shop, they had known who she was, but nobody had taken the time to get to know her. No one had claimed to be her friend. Duke couldn't figure out if that was due to her personality or the lack of time she'd been in town. She'd been working at the cafe for three months before she disappeared. Everyone assumed she had up and left town without a word goodbye. Because the place she'd been renting had been cleared of her stuff. Why else would they think anything bad had happened? She took all her belongings with her. People had rented after her, so trying to pull prints was a useless endeavor.

Now Duke knew the killer had made it look like she left on a whim.

The body had been submerged in the lake for a year, presuming the killer had tossed her in the lake the day she died. It had wiped away any viable evidence. What the medical examiner could infer was she'd been strangled. Determining if she'd been raped beforehand had been too difficult to pin down due to the deterioration of her body. The killer had tied a rope around her feet that was attached to a slate block. Too bad for the killer, the rope had somehow broken, which was how her body floated to the top. They might not have ever found her if not for that.

So with no evidence, no witnesses seeing her leave town, no idea if she had a problem with anyone, Duke had nowhere to go with the case.

Stone cold.

Yet, he couldn't let it go.

He'd removed all the photos and documentation he'd built up—which wasn't a whole lot—from the conference room at the precinct and brought it home. Now he had it all set up in his spare room. Every morning before he left for work, he stared it. Bore a hole in the wall, he stared so hard and for so long.

Nothing new ever jumped out. Not that he expected something to appear before him. But it helped him cope with the feeling that he'd failed this woman. A woman he hadn't even known that well.

She'd been a lost soul that ventured into town, and she'd

remain one until he found her killer. Found her the justice she deserved.

He had figured Juliet, her employer from Noel's Cafe, would have had most of the answers he wanted. But even Juliet hadn't known much about her. And in typical Juliet fashion, she hadn't bothered to do a background check or call any of the references that Beth had given her. When Duke took the time to do so, they all came back fake. Beth had lied up and down her application. If Juliet—

Damn it!

He wasn't going to let his mind wander to that place. Blaming Juliet wasn't going to help him solve the case. She saw a woman in need, and that's all she needed to see to hire her. Juliet had a heart of gold. She'd help anyone who needed it. She had obviously seen something in Beth's eyes to think she had needed help.

So the big question was why Beth had chosen to lie about herself? What had she been hiding?

When he'd run a check in the police database, he found no criminal record, not even a speeding ticket. While she might've lied about her references, she had given her real name. Her driver's license wasn't fake. That just brought more questions than answers. Why lie about her references then? The address on her license had been a location in New York. That last-known address hadn't proven to be helpful in the least. She'd had it marked as her residence, but when he'd called the location, she hadn't lived there for over two years. So odd. Who was this woman? Why had she lied about everything?

The place she rented didn't even have her last-known address. He wasn't sure why Mindy, the previous realtor of the town, hadn't done more of a background check on her either. It shouldn't have mattered Beth had been renting month by month. A history of her should've been done. To make sure she *could* make the rent each month. But Duke shouldn't have been surprised. Not when Mindy's brother had been revealed to be a predator of the truly sick variety. Putting cameras in the places she managed, spying on the residents. It had never been proven, nor had Mindy or her brother admitted to it, but he wouldn't be surprised if Mindy had helped him do his dirty work.

Beth was a ghost. A mystery he wanted to solve.

The worse part—besides not finding who killed her— was he was unable to notify her family. If she even had a family. What must they be wondering about her?

They'd buried Beth's body in the cemetery plot in a small section away from people who grew up and lived their life and then died in town. Maybe because he felt bad for failing her, he visited her on occasion. He didn't stay long or say much, but it made him feel better letting her know he hadn't given up on her.

Because he was as bad as the rest of the town.

He hadn't taken the time to get to know her either. A smile here, a thanks there when he ventured into the cafe to purchase something and she happened to be working. But that was it. He hadn't bothered to chat with her.

Shit. If he didn't get going, he'd be late for work.

Pushing all thoughts of Beth out of his mind, he filled his coffee mug one more time, gulping half of it before he even walked out the door.

His first stop was to Mocha's Merriment for another cup of coffee. Not that he needed a third cup, but he liked supporting the local shops. Lila had done wonders this past summer building their town's reputation back to some of its former glory. With a freshly found dead body in the mix, it was a damn miracle how well she did. Halloween was a week away and the rental properties around town were full. The town was brimming with tourists, and with Christmas around the corner, it would stay that way—hopefully.

But despite all that, he always supported the local shops as much as he could. Because tides could turn and they could be back to scraping by.

Griffin was in his office when he got to the precinct. He always liked stopping by to say hi to his best friend, and the chief of police.

"How's it going this morning?" he asked in lieu of a greeting, knocking on the open door.

Griffin looked up from the paperwork plastered across his desk. "Excellent. I plan to meet with Bryce and Lila later today to go over the details of the parade one last time. They are not accepting any more floats and whatnot, which is a damn good thing. This parade is going to last two to three hours with the amount that signed up. It's insane."

Duke chuckled. "Lila is a genius. That's why."

They'd never had a Halloween parade before. Thanksgiving, yes. Fourth of July, yes. Christmas, sometimes. That one was a tossup. Not everyone liked to sit outside in the freezing cold watching floats go by. The few times they tried it, it'd been pretty much a failure. Knowing Lila, she'd try again this year and it'd be a banging success.

"That she is." Griffin leaned back in his chair. "Hey, you coming over tonight for supper and game night?"

In the last two months, the Stuarts had started game night on Fridays. Duke wasn't sure who started it, but it had happened on Friday and then kept happening. Now it was a weekly tradition. Griffin and Eve were partners. Of course, Bryce and Lila always paired up. That left him and Juliet together. It was awkward. Because he'd loved her for most of his life and she had never seen him as more than a brother.

Why the hell was he always invited anyway? He wasn't a Stuart.

Well, that was easy to decipher. He was best friends with Griffin. Being an only child, he'd always been in the mix with the Stuarts growing up. Nothing had changed there.

"I think I have to pass this week." Like he passed the last two Fridays.

"Well, hey, if you change your mind, your seat is always there."

"I know that. Thanks, Grif. I'm going to head out on patrol, unless you need me to do anything."

"We're good. Have a nice day."

He returned the sentiment and left the precinct.

How had his life come to this?

A dismal officer that couldn't solve a murder.

A friend who must look so pathetic he was invited to family game night when he wasn't family.

A guy who pined over a woman who would never see him as more.

Hell, no!

He was not going down to pity town. He would not do that to himself. The murder case wasn't his fault. What was he to do when there was no evidence? And Griffin was his best friend. He'd been invited to everything the Stuarts always did. Griffin wasn't treating him any different. There was no pity involved.

And as for Juliet. He'd come to terms with never having a chance last winter when Aster, Lila's brother, strolled into town. It had opened his eyes that Juliet would never see him as a potential suitor. Not when someone like Aster captured her attention right away.

So that meant he had to stop wallowing in his own self-pity and forget all about her.

Get back into the dating game.

SHE LET GO of the handle of her suitcase. It wobbled, then toppled to the side with a loud thud. Whatever. The one wheel on the left side had been broken for...she couldn't remember, and it happened all the time. Nothing had ever broken inside because she packed well. Not that she ever packed anything breakable either. But if she had, it wouldn't have broken from the fall.

"It's small."

She looked at her brother with a wide grin. "But's it cute. And quaint."

He rolled his eyes. "We're not here for cute and quaint."

She shut the door, ignoring his whiny attitude. He'd been like that from the moment they left the house, all through the airport, and the entire drive to the tiny town of Sleighville.

The cottage she found to rent was small. She couldn't disagree. The front door opened to the living room where she could see the kitchen right behind it. A dining room next to it, if one could call it that. There was a table in the kitchen, so maybe it was more classified as a nook. There was a small hallway that led to the right. Her brother disappeared down that way.

"You have got to be shitting me!"

So he planned on whining the entire time they were here. Great. At least he had come with. Otherwise, she'd be doing all of this on her own. Deep down, she wasn't sure she'd be able to do it on her own. Not that she'd ever admit that to him. One word of worry and he'd make her leave.

He strolled back into the room, glowering. "There's one bedroom."

Oh, well, that wasn't good.

"Seriously?"

"Yeah," he drawled with sarcasm. "One bedroom. I am not sharing a bed with my sister!"

She threw her hands up in the air. "Well, no one asked you to come with. I'm sorry the cottage is so damn small and only has one bed! I didn't have time to ask the realtor for two beds because when I told her I wanted to rent something, she only had this one left! I had no choice, asshole!"

During her entire tirade, she had walked closer to him, shoving past him as the last word left her mouth. Even the damn hallway was short. She slammed the bathroom door for extra measure. He had no right to be mad at her. Not at any point when she told him her plans had she asked him to join her. In fact, it was the last thing she wanted. For a moment, she had regretted telling him.

Until she dismissed that notion. She had to tell someone where she was going. Lest her dead body wash up on shore too.

And despite how angry she felt, she knew he had to be here. She couldn't do this alone. She didn't *want* to do this alone. But again, she'd never admit that to him.

A soft knock sounded on the door.

"I'm sorry. I'm an ass."

Yeah, he was.

A colossal one.

"Come on. Open the door and forgive me. It's not a big deal. I'll sleep on the couch."

No doubt in her mind that's what would happen. Because she sure in the hell wasn't. Not when this was her idea to begin with.

She grabbed the knob and twisted, opening the door to see the sincerity in his face.

"You know I yell when I get scared. I'm really scared." He clutched her shoulders. "I'm not sure this was a great idea."

"It's the only idea we have."

She placed her hands over his, patting them to reassure him, then removed them. "I need a drink. Anything. Food would be good too. We should've stopped at a fast-food joint before coming here." Not that she'd seen any commercial fast-food places. Everything in town looked to be local joints, not allowing the big corporations in.

They'd gotten off the plane, picked up the rental car, and hit the road to Sleighville, stopping by the realtor's office to get the key to the cottage and directions, and came straight here. She was hungry, which always put her in a dangerous mood. They had barely eaten yesterday either. Her nerves had been too ramped up for much. Though, to be fair, she'd been out of whack and not herself for a few weeks. Her brother was her rock. He kept her grounded and sane when she wanted to forget the world and everything in it. She would've fallen apart if not for him. She knew it, and he knew it. Not that he ever rubbed that knowledge in her face.

"Right. That's a great idea. There's no food here. So let's go find a place to eat and then buy some groceries. Come back here and make a game plan." He cocked a brow. "You do have a game plan, right?"

No. She had no plan whatsoever.

"Of course."

Not that she'd confess the truth to her brother. He was already pissed she wanted to come here.

A knock sounded on the front door.

"Expecting company?"

Her brother was going to get on her nerves. "We just got

here. Can you, at least, wait a full day before acting like an annoying imbecile?"

She didn't expect a response and didn't get one as she passed him and opened the door. A pretty woman with shoulder-length auburn hair stood with a plate of cookies. Shaped from Halloween cutouts: bats, ghosts, a witch hat, pumpkins, and a cat. Except they were frosted with Christmas cheer. Red and green on all of them, giving them a very merry vibe. It was an odd combination, but they looked delicious.

"Hi. I'm Eve. I live next door. I saw the car in the driveway and figured someone had rented it. I wanted to welcome you to Sleighville, and I hope you have a wonderful time here."

Wow. She hadn't expected this. Talk about friendly. None of her neighbors had ever knocked on her door before. Not even to borrow sugar or something weird like that.

"Umm, thanks. Appreciate the welcome." She honestly had no idea what to say.

"I made cookies." Eve giggled, her cheeks dusting a rosy red. "Not in the span of five minutes. I mean, I made them earlier and planned to bring them to town, but I thought I'd bring a few over to you as a welcome gift." She held out the plate.

"Thank you. They look delicious."

"Yeah, they do." Her brother grabbed the plate from her, unwrapping the saran wrap from around them, and gobbled one up like the pig he could be. "Oh, these are amazing."

Then he walked away with the cookies toward the kitchen. She couldn't have been more embarrassed.

"I'm sorry. It's been a long day of traveling. He normally has better manners."

Eve smiled, though the way she darted glances behind her shoulder at her brother was odd. "Of course. Well, welcome. I'm right next door. If you need me. For anything."

Okay. Even more odd. The way Eve said it with such seriousness.

"Appreciate it."

Then she waved goodbye before closing the door. As she walked toward the kitchen to try a cookie herself, she realized she never introduced herself or her brother. She doubted that would be the last time she saw the woman. How rude. She'd have to rectify her mistake because the people of this town needed to like and trust them.

Oh, man. The cookies *were* delicious. Like, melt in your mouth, eat the whole plate kind of delicious. She ate three before they left.

They got back into the car and drove to Main Street where he found a spot to park right in front of a cafe. Laughter filled the vehicle.

"Look at that shit! I love it."

She pursed her lips, not amused as she read the sign "Noel's Cafe" in big bold festive letters. The Christmas lights dangling from the eve didn't bother her as much as the sign.

"You're going to fit right in," he mused. "*Noel*."

"Yeah, so are you, jolly St. *Nick*."

It was just their luck to have to travel to a town that celebrated Christmas year-round, especially with the names Noel and Nick. It was like a cruel joke had been played on them by their sister. Not that she had planned any of this. Noel knew that.

Nick's jovial attitude disappeared. "You know this was where she worked before she disappeared."

Noel knew. She'd read all the newspaper clippings she could find, grabbing as much information as she could before deciding she had to come. Plus, her brother had done his research as well. He hadn't been happy sharing his findings with her. Always the protector, trying to look out for her. But she had insisted, and he couldn't keep it from her.

God, she was so glad he decided to come with her. Being alone, she'd fall apart sooner or later, but not with him right by her side. They had come to do one thing, and she would not fail in her mission.

They'd come to Sleighville to find out who murdered their sister Beth.

"So it's a good place to start our investigation."

Nick grabbed her arm, though not enough to hurt her. But enough to let her feel the fear he had.

"We don't know what happened to Beth. We don't even know why she left us. I lost one sister, and I'm sure in the hell not losing another one. We do all of this my way. I don't want you poking your nose into shit here."

She shook his arm off. "Nick, that is the reason we came. To poke our nose in shit. I'm not leaving it all to you. Again, I will remind you I didn't ask you to come with."

But she was soooo damn glad he insisted he join her.

He scoffed. "Like I was going to let you come on your own when you told me. You're damn lucky you told me too."

"Feed me before I rip your head off."

"Fine."

Noel noticed Eve walk into the cafe as she got out of the car. Was the woman following them? Things were off about that woman.

Of course, the whole town was off.

It celebrated Christmas year-round.

And someone in this merry town had killed her sister.

2

———

Duke's gaze left the couple that were exiting a vehicle to greet Eve as she strolled up to his table.

"I hear you're not coming tonight."

Oh, this was the part where they tried to make him feel guilty. Because they felt sorry for him. Being all alone.

Or so he imagined. He didn't truly think they felt sorry for him. But deep down inside, he felt sorry for himself.

"Yeah, not tonight." He wasn't going into any reason why.

Eve didn't dig further, and he didn't think she would. She liked her privacy, so she always respected other people's privacy as well.

The bell above the door dinged as the couple strolled in. The man had a rough, don't-mess-with-me look to him. Broad shouldered. Very fit male. Short brown hair and a face he figured most women would swoon over. The woman also had brown hair, darker and longer, and a pretty face. Nothing too beautiful where men would fight over her, but pretty enough that she was taken. But with the rough and tumble guy she was with. She had a nice figure that also suggested she worked out to maintain her physique. The sweater she wore molded to her figure. Definitely more muscle hiding under her clothes rather than fat. Something he wouldn't mind confirming. And she had a nice set of breasts—he was male, he couldn't help but look—and an ass worth grabbing.

Damn!

Yeah, it was time to start dating again. Imagining the things he was about a random woman was not normal. He needed to get laid, if nothing else. It'd been too long.

"You see that man and woman?" Eve whispered, leaning closer to him.

"I do."

"They rented the cottage next to us."

Okay. He waited for Eve to add whatever was bothering her.

"You know I like to welcome people to town. I like to make everyone feel welcome and that this is a happy and safe place."

No doubt that helped with tourism as well. Word of mouth was the best kind of advertisement.

"I was walking across the yard with a plate of cookies when I heard shouting." Eve shivered, remembering things from her own past she didn't want to remember.

She'd had an abusive brother that damn near killed her. Duke knew there were things she didn't want to ever think about again. Juliet had also been abused by her ex-husband. Both women would step in and help anyone who looked to be in danger because they had lived it themselves.

"The woman answered the door." She puckered her brows. "I forgot to get her name. But anyway, she seemed okay. The guy was...sort of rude. Can you keep an eye on them for me?"

Definitely. He always grabbed a high-top table near the

window so he could watch the coming and goings while he had his lunch. He'd noticed the moment the man parked. He also noticed how he'd grabbed her arm.

"You know I will. Don't worry, Eve."

"Thank you, Duke. I'll let you get back to your meal. And please, rethink coming to game night. It won't be the same without you."

Doubtful, but he didn't respond. Just smiled. Eve walked away and ventured to the back of the cafe out of view.

Duke watched the couple looking at the options before deciding on the special of the day. Turkey club sandwich with a bowl of tomato basil soup. Good choice. He'd had the same thing and it had been wonderful. Every last bite. They took a seat on the opposite side of the cafe from him, but near the window.

The woman dug in, scarfing down her food as if she hadn't eaten in days. The man took his time. Was he withholding food from her? How odd. Though, Duke could appreciate a woman who enjoyed food and wasn't afraid of eating anything. He'd dated one woman that had to know every last ingredient before she took one bite. Most of the time, she declined because it wasn't something she wanted to put in her body. That relationship had lasted a month.

Hell. His longest relationship had to be three...maybe four months. He liked to think it wasn't because of Juliet, but deep in the back of his mind, he knew she had played a part. He unfairly judged them all based off her. When they didn't meet his expectations, he dropped them.

From this day forward, he'd stop that. No one could live up to Juliet because they were each their own woman. And if he stopped to look at Juliet, he knew he'd find some faults that aggravated him.

Or not.

He was trying to get over the fact nothing would ever happen between them.

The couple leaned closer together across from each other, as if whispering. The woman didn't look happy.

So they were arguing.

Again.

Duke stood up, cleared his table and threw the garbage away, and put his dishware in the appropriate spot.

It was time to introduce himself.

He walked up to the table with a friendly expression. When the woman noticed him, her eyes flashed a moment of fear, before masking it. But he'd seen it.

"Good afternoon, folks. Welcome to Sleighville." His uniform was enough to inform them he worked for the police department. "First day in town?"

His question should tell them he kept an eye on everything. He knew it was their first day in town. But he wanted to make them feel better by phrasing it as a question.

"Just drove in today," the man responded. "Cute town."

"We aim to please." Duke shifted his stance, resting his hand on the butt of his gun while maintaining eye contact with the guy. Give him a small warning he shouldn't mess around while in this town. "I'm Officer Duke Fisk. I wanted to introduce myself, welcome you to town." He paused. "And you fine folks are?"

"Thanks for the warm welcome," the guy said with a short laugh. "Chick next door to us did the same thing." He wiped his hand on his thigh before holding it out to Duke. "Nick Lancaster." Then he gestured to the woman. "Noel."

Duke met her gaze when he heard her name.

She had a soft, airy laughter. "I know. Crazy, right? One of the reasons Nick and I couldn't resist visiting the town."

They were odd names. If they were fake, not very bright

to use names associated with Christmas. One quick check in the system would show if they were lying.

"I like it." His attention lingered on her longer than he should've. "Both of your names, I mean. Make sure you stop at Tidings and Joy Apparel. Shannon gives out a free shirt to every new visitor. Another warm welcome from the town."

"Really? That is super nice," Noel said, then looked at Nick. "We're so stopping there."

The man resisted rolling his eyes. If Duke hadn't been watching him like a hawk he would've missed the subtle gesture.

"Well, I won't keep you. If you need anything, you know where to find me." Duke made sure to look at Noel when he said it.

Because if she needed help from this man, all she had to do was go to the police station. He'd take care of her problem in a heartbeat.

She nodded but said nothing.

He bid his goodbyes, waved to Theresa behind the counter, and left.

To wander around the town and hope no serious issues popped up. He already had one unsolved murder on his shoulders. He didn't need another.

NICK LEANED TOWARD HER, whispering, "That was weird. Why was that cop over here?"

She giggled, shoving the last bite into her mouth, chewing and talking as best she could. "It's a small town, Nick. They operate way different than a big city. I'm sure he does that with every new visitor he sees."

She wouldn't have minded staring at him a bit longer.

The man was hot with a capital T. Short black hair, and styled enough in a certain way that it could be mussed up with a quick flick of her hand. Two cute dimples when he smiled. And damn! The man's smile could blind a woman with desire. Talk about filling out a uniform. His butt was even nice, stretching those pants, making a woman want to take notice. And deep-blue eyes that she felt penetrated straight to her soul, as if searching for all her secrets. His stare had unnerved her a bit. Though, she was on edge to begin with.

Her brother snapped his fingers in her face. "Where did you go?"

Drooling over a man in uniform. So sue her!

"Thinking about what to order next so I can interview that lady behind the counter. You didn't give me much of a chance earlier."

"You need to tread carefully here, Noel. You can't just up and start asking questions about a dead woman."

She stood up, shoving her chair behind her. "You can be such an ass." Lowering closer to his ear, she hissed, "She was our sister. Not just a dead woman."

Noel tossed her trash away and put the plate and bowl in the area next to the garbage can, then walked up to the counter. The woman—her name tag said it was Theresa—smiled with a greeting.

"I'm still hungry, I could eat a horse. That sandwich and soup was delicious."

"I'll be sure to let Juliet know. She owns the cafe."

Noel pointed at the treats behind the display case. "And which dessert should I be munching on now?"

Theresa blew out a mixture of a large breath and laughter. "Do not make me pick. They are all good. Eve, our master baker, can't get anything wrong."

"Oh, does she work here? We're renting the place next to her, and she brought us cookies. I've never tasted anything so good."

"Right!" Theresa leaned on the display case, laughing. "I swear she has magic in her hands."

"You know what? If you can't choose, I can't choose. I already said I could eat a horse. Bag me up one of everything."

Theresa's eyes grew large. "Seriously?"

"Don't let this figure fool you. I can eat. Me and food have the best relationship."

"Girl, don't I know it," Theresa answered as if she had the same problem. Though she didn't show signs that the food made one part of her body larger than another.

Noel made sure she worked out, and not because she didn't want to put on weight. Because it was a part of her. A routine she'd establish as a young girl. Once a person had a routine down, it was hard to break it.

She paid—an astronomical price—for the food, thanked Theresa, telling her she'd be seeing her sooner rather than later, and they left.

"Why did you buy every damn thing there?" Nick asked once they were in the car away from prying ears.

"You don't want me coming right out and asking questions about Beth, so I'm doing it the hard way. Trying to make friends so they'll dish out the information easier."

"We're going to be here forever," Nick mumbled as he drove away.

They spent the day exploring the town, meeting new people, walking into every shop. Noel made sure to chat with as many people as she could. Even got her free shirt. A bunch of jolly elves dancing around a Christmas tree filled with presents. The tree had actual lights on it. And when she pressed the button to light it up, it even sang "have a holly jolly christmas." She couldn't believe Shannon gave it away for free. Before they left town, she'd have to search for more fun, annoying shirts. Because Nick had already hollered at her several times to stop pushing the damn button.

In all her interactions, she never mentioned Beth. She didn't bring up a death occurred in town. She didn't pry in any gossip or secrets the town held. That would come in time. Soon, all these people would be her best friend and would share without her even asking. She'd be one of them.

She'd make sure of it.

Nick made supper—steaks on the stove. They weren't horrible, but they weren't great. Considering he forgot to get charcoal when he bought them, he couldn't grill them outside like they had planned.

It was chilly out, so she wasn't complaining. And she hadn't felt obligated to sit outside with him while he grilled.

By the time nine o'clock rolled around, Nick was snoring on the couch. The man could never stay awake past eight half the time when they traveled. And after three beers, nope. He was out like a log. Snoring like a grizzly bear.

She'd had one beer. Nursed it too.

So she'd be okay to drive.

She made sure not to make a sound as she closed the door behind her and locked it. Frost's Pub and Grill looked busy for a Friday night, as it should. Tables were filled with talkative and laughing people. The two pool tables in the corner had lively games going on. The bar was also filled from one end to the other. Though, she managed to find a spot in the corner on the opposite end from the entrance. It gave her a great view of the whole place. She liked knowing what was in front of her—and behind her. A nice, solid wall.

She took her light jacket off and placed it behind the chair, hanging her purse on the hook under the bar.

A man strolled from one end of the bar to her side, tossing down a napkin. "Welcome to Sleighville. What can I get you to drink?"

"A nice cold beer for now. House special. I don't care. I need something cold."

The beer appeared a second later and the first drink went down her throat in a satisfying way.

"I'm Anton. You are...Noel."

She nearly spit out her second sip. "How do you know that?"

Anton leaned on the bar with his forearm, producing a cocky grin that made her pulse skip a beat. She had to admit this town was packed with hot men. Maybe that's what had been Beth's downfall. Which wrong man did she pick?

"Well, see, word spreads quickly. We love tourists. Keeps us in business. And you and your hubby walked up and down Main Street visiting everyone but me. I felt left out."

Her hubby?

O. M. G.

This town thought Nick was her husband. Gross!

"I apologize for my oversight earlier. I am here now, and the night isn't over, so I didn't skip you. I waited to save the best for last."

Anton burst out laughing, pointing a finger at her. "You're going to be trouble. I feel it in my bones." He winked at her. "That's my favorite kind of woman." Then he left to help another customer.

Favorite kind of woman, uh? What else did he like about a woman? Had he liked Beth? Did he tease and flirt with Beth like he did with her? These were all questions she wanted to ask but couldn't. Not yet.

She hadn't inserted herself into the town much. But soon.

"You're alone."

Noel twisted her head to see Officer Duke Fisk right next to her. Not in a uniform either. It didn't matter what the man wore—currently a black T-shirt and faded blue jeans—it all fit him well.

And her pulse that had ratcheted up with Anton skyrocketed when Duke flashed her a smile. Those two adorable dimples did something to her. Made her stomach flutter like a bunch of butterflies trying to break free. His deep-deep-blue eyes sparkled with mischief. She could get lost in those eyes.

Anton thought she was trouble.

Then this man was her perfect match in that category.

3

SHE HADN'T RESPONDED to his ridiculous greeting. *You're alone.* Why did he start with that? Of course, he did want to know where her boyfriend was. Or husband. The buzz around town couldn't decide since he had on a ring and she did not.

"I am." She feigned looking around him. "You appear to be alone too."

He had no chair to sit down on, so he scooted closer in between her and the guy sitting on the stool next to her, leaning on the bar. He liked how it brought him a little too close to her. She didn't react much to his nearness except for a sharp inhale of breath.

"Technically, but I know most people here, so not truly alone."

"Like me, you're insinuating."

He winced. "I didn't mean to make that sound like an insult. I apologize."

She touched his shoulder and the desire he'd felt for her earlier, surged. He wanted her hands somewhere else on his body. Desperately.

What was wrong with him? He never reacted to someone he just met like this. Especially an out-of-towner.

"You're forgiven. I was messing with you."

Then her hand fell back to the bar and his heart plummeted.

Since when did he get so hard over a woman he just met? Because his cock was at full attention right now. The moment she'd placed her hand on him.

He'd done his normal rounds in town, meeting new people everywhere he went. Thanks to Lila and her reeling in tourists. None of them had set his blood on fire like this woman. There was something different about her. Something he couldn't quite put his finger on.

And she was married.

"Where's your husband?"

She snorted, spewing out the beer she'd taken a sip of. "Sorry. That was embarrassing." She grabbed napkins from a holder near her, wiping up her mess. Even tried soaking up some of it that hit her shirt.

A plain white T-shirt, V-cut, that showed him too much of her breasts, making him ache to glide a finger from the mound to one of her perky nipples. And he could see her nipples, or at least the hardness of them. Part of the wetness had hit that area, showcasing it more than he wanted it to. She looked like she had a pink bra on underneath the white shirt.

"I misspoke? Boyfriend, then."

"Eww to both of those. He's my brother."

Well, that changed things in his favor.

"Oh. My bad. I misread the situation."

And he'd assumed they were married along with everyone else when he'd ran their names and found they had the same last name. It never occurred to him they were brother and sister. Not when the guy had been so possessive with her.

It should've occurred to him. Eve had dealt with an abusive brother. It was known to happen.

"You're forgiven." Her lips turned up into a beautiful grin, her chestnut-colored eyes twinkling with merriment. "Again."

He knew they hadn't lied about their names either. Unless they knew how to hack the system and create fake profiles of themselves. No criminal record for either of them. Not even a traffic ticket.

"So were your parents lovers of Christmas?"

She rolled her eyes. "Don't get me started on our names." Her brow rose in the air. "How does one get the name Duke?"

He chuckled. "Easy. When your mother loves historical romances. When she can't pick her favorite fictional duke, she gives the name of Duke so it could mean any one of them."

She leaned closer, the laughter sparkling in her dark, hazel eyes. "You're kidding, right?"

"God, I wish I was."

She placed her hand on his shoulder again, and he soaked up the small touch. "I love that for you. It's the best story I've ever heard."

"Now you return the favor. Give me a spectacular story." He bopped her nose with a gentle touch of his finger. It was silly, but it ramped up the ache settling in his gut.

"Okay, fine. Twist my finger. Yes, my mom was a lover of the holiday. Believe it or not, my birthday is Christmas Eve. Trust me, it's not fun. And Nick's is the day after Christmas. I shit you not, I'm pretty sure she tried her hardest to make it fall on Christmas Day, and nearly accomplished her goal for both of us."

He'd noticed that in his background search of them and couldn't come up with a believable explanation for it. Unless they had created fake identities. It was so outrageous, it was hard to believe. Yet, he didn't doubt her story.

"So why isn't your mom with you two?"

The happiness in her expression vanished for the first time as she looked away, fiddling with her beer. "She passed away when we were kids."

"Shit, Noel. I'm sorry."

"Yeah, me too."

"Do you like Christmas then?"

She shrugged, their earlier banter not feeling the same. "It's a holiday like any other, I guess. It comes and goes without much fanfare. How about you? What's it like living here year-round?"

"Well, I moved here when I was five, so I've been here all my life. You get used to it. It's another small town, except you see Christmas everywhere you go."

"And you don't get sick of it?"

"Not really. I don't know any different."

Stilted silence filtered through the small space. He hated it. He didn't know where to go from here. Pining over Juliet hadn't done him any favors since her divorce. He'd held out hope she'd see him as more than a friend. Of course, he never made it obvious he liked her. Asking her out would've helped. But he'd done little dating in a long while, and it was showing.

"Hey, Duke. Need a refill?"

Anton appeared out of nowhere, and he appreciated the break in the silence.

"Yeah, thanks."

"And how about you?" Anton asked Noel as he grabbed a beer from the cooler near him and handed it to Duke.

"Are you trying to get me drunk, Anton?" She wagged her finger in his face. "I just started this beer."

"Hey, I'm getting to know you. You're not a fast drinker. Duly noted." He tapped his head as if telling her he was storing the information.

Then Anton was gone, helping more customers.

"He's a flirt."

Duke chuckled. "He is, but he's harmless. He never mixes business with pleasure."

She twisted her body more in line with his, leaning her elbow on the bar and propping her hand to her head. "You're telling me, you know, without a doubt, he's never taken a woman home after a shift."

Duke nodded. "Without a doubt. Anton's a first-class guy. He's here to make you happy. Make money." He looked at her beer bottle. "He's also here to make sure you're safe from other patrons who might be looking for trouble. He can't do that if he's getting goo-goo eyes over someone. He may appear to be flirting, but he's being nice."

She winced. "Ouch."

He ran his words back through his mind, then matched her wince. He'd made it sound like Anton was playing games to make a buck. "I made that sound bad at the end. He's an idiot if he's not flirting with you."

She ran a finger down his chest. "Are you now flirting with me to make up for that subtle insult?"

He took a swallow of his beer to prevent himself from leaning closer to her. "Maybe."

The gorgeous smile that lit up her face had his cock springing to life again. She *wanted* him to be flirting with her.

"But not to make up for any accidental insult."

He had to make that clarification. He was attracted to her. Had been from the moment he saw her walk into the cafe. And he wasn't quite sure it was just because he'd had a long drought of sex.

"So tell me more about this wonderful town." She ran another finger down his chest. "And you."

He was more than happy to keep the conversation flowing. Not much to be said about the town. They celebrated Christmas year-round. The townsfolk loved to gossip, but would help anyone out for any reason. Of course, he made sure to avoid any talk of murder. That included the unsolved one that recently occurred and the death of Bryce's wife that had shaken the town to the core. One of their own beloved —Becca—had surprised them all, killing his wife in a fit of rage.

He kind of glossed over his life as well as there wasn't much to say. Nothing exciting anyway. He grew up here. Loved baseball and collecting rare coins. He didn't go to college, but went right into law enforcement and worked his way to being the chief of police's right-hand man. Though, that had more to do with him being best friends with Griffin. He trusted him, and vice versa.

Her bottle looked as empty as his as time passed.

"Can I buy you another drink?"

She eyed her bottle, biting her bottom lip. "One. I have to drive home." He went to raise his hand to motion for Anton when she lowered it. "I have to use the restroom first."

The devious glint in her eyes as she stood up, and the way she dragged her finger across his shoulder as she walked past told him he was supposed to follow.

But what could happen in the bar?

There were people everywhere.

His mind was playing tricks on him, wanting something that wasn't going to happen tonight. Plus, he didn't sleep with women he barely knew. Never had he done something so outrageous. Call him old-fashioned but he liked a few dates before he took a woman to bed.

When five minutes had passed, he decided it was his duty to check on her. The hallway was empty when he ventured toward the bathroom.

So she was still in the bathroom. No need to worry.

The door opened before he could turn around and return to the bar.

"Are you following me?"

He couldn't hold back his grin, not when she looked at him with her own sly one. "No. I—no." Hell, he didn't know how to explain why he followed her. So yeah, he had lied.

She held his gaze, her lips curling up as the seconds passed by. He wasn't sure if it was the smile that reeled him in or an invisible force that couldn't keep him away.

He stepped closer, brought his hand up, brushing her cheek, and kissed her.

OH, boy. This kiss ranked up to the top ten she'd ever had. As his tongue dove in, doing delicious things she didn't know a tongue could do, she decided it had to be top five instead. His hands wrapped around her, clutching her waist, pinning her to the wall.

The kiss didn't stop. If anything, the barrier holding her in place intensified the kiss to a dangerous level.

He grinded into her and she moaned at the contact. It had been so long since she'd done this. After the last loser she dated, she had sworn off men until she was forty. Considering that was ten years away, it had been a delusion from the onset.

"Damn, I want you, Noel." He broke the kiss to whisper the plea against her lips.

She answered with a resounding, "yes." Though it came out more in a low murmur, almost an aching moan.

One second they were in the hallway, bright lights surrounding them. The next she was in a dark room, their breathing the only sound they could hear.

Duke flipped a light switch, letting her know he'd maneuvered them into a supply closet that must've been close to the bathroom.

She was backed against the wall next to the door, yet he wasn't doing anything but staring at her.

She'd had one beer before she left for the bar. One beer while she was here. In no way was she drunk and incapable of making a bad decision. While she didn't know how many he had before he walked up to her, she didn't think he had that many either. His eyes weren't glossy or glazed over. Not like she'd witnessed too many times in her life to know the difference between drunk and sober.

"Noel..."

They were in here now. While she had time to walk away from whatever was about to happen, she didn't want to. She always lived life with too many precautions, always afraid of getting hurt. Why not live for once, not worry about the consequences? Let herself have fun for once in her life.

Before he could finish whatever he couldn't say, her hand trailed to his jeans, unbuckling his belt and then undoing the button. He inhaled sharply but didn't stop her. The zipper slid down and her hand dove in, wrapping around his hard cock.

His eyes closed as he groaned in pleasure. "Oh, yes. Don't stop." Then his hands were on her pants, removing the barrier that kept him away from touching her. He shoved her pants down halfway, touching her in the right spot on the first try. His finger slid in as she stroked him with slow easy strokes.

Then they were kissing again.

Tongues dueling.

Hands groping and stroking in unison.

But it wasn't enough.

She knew it wasn't for him either. Because his free hand guided her pants down until they hit the floor, making it easier for her to step out of her shoes and out of the pants. In the same movement, she was shoving his pants farther down as well.

He paused for a moment, shuffling his hand behind him. Then the crinkle of a package told her he'd taken out a condom he carried in his wallet.

Then his hand was replacing hers on his cock. He lifted her up and plunged deep inside. A loud moan, close to a scream, would've escaped her lips if he hadn't resumed kissing her.

She wrapped her legs around his waist as he pounded in and out of her, holding her against the wall. At no point did she feel like he would drop her. She felt safe and secure in his arms.

The twist of their lips with the thrusting of his hips sent her to a place she didn't think she'd ever been. Sex was sex. But this? This was primal. Feral in a way. Dirty, naughty sex that she'd never had.

She loved it.

And it was nearing the end. Way too soon. She felt the

pleasure rising to the surface. When it hit her, she bit his lip —unintentionally, but it happened nonetheless.

He thrusted several more times before groaning in bliss, tensing and shuddering in her arms.

"Shit."

What every woman wanted to hear after the best sex of her life.

"Give me a moment, Noel." He bent his head, peppering a few kisses on her neck as his breathing slowed to a normal pace. "I didn't hurt you, did I?"

She rubbed his back in a soothing gesture. "No. Why would you think so? If anyone hurt anyone, I did. I bit your lip. I'm sorry."

His cerulean-blue eyes reappeared before her and she couldn't quite read them. "No apologies necessary. I've never had sex against a wall before." His brows drew low. "Or in a bar."

She wanted to giggle at his distraught expression, but her lips held it in. "That makes two of us."

He blew out a slow breath, looking in pain for a moment, before disengaging and letting her feet hit the floor.

Awkward silence filled the room as they fixed their clothing.

"You are still buying me that beer, aren't you?"

He held a dirty condom in his hand, since there wasn't a garbage nearby, and the sight made her giggle.

"I most certainly am."

"Good. You dispose of that," she said, flicking a finger at the condom, giggling some more. "I'll go make sure our seats weren't taken."

"Yes, ma'am."

There. It didn't have to be awkward between them. So

they had sex. Had the most mind-blowing sex ever, but it didn't have to be weird.

She left the supply closet first, grateful no one else was in the hallway, and took her seat. No one had taken it. And shit! She'd left her purse unattended. That was a mistake. That man made her lose her senses, forget everything around her.

Anton appeared out of nowhere. "I thought you might've left."

Without her coat or purse? Never. She wasn't that clueless.

"No. Bathroom break." A really long bathroom break.

Duke was suddenly by her side. "One more round, Anton."

Anton tilted his head. "I thought you left too."

"Phone call."

Duke said it so smoothly, even she believed him. Anton grabbed their beers and left them alone. Duke stood more behind her this time as the guy in the stool next to her had crowded the space more. He thought they had left as well. She shivered when Duke's lips hit the back of her neck.

"I had a nice time tonight."

So did she.

They finished their beers faster than she would've liked, chatting about inconsequential things the rest of the time. Of course, when she was ready to leave, he walked her to the car. She wasn't sure if that was the gentleman in him or the officer part of him. Probably a bit of both.

"Drive safe." Then he kissed her goodbye, making her wish he had offered to drive her back to his place.

But as she drove home, this had been the better decision. She had a goal here. One goal.

Find who killed her sister.

Sleeping with an officer was not one of them.

The lights were out when she pulled into the driveway. Whew. Nick hadn't woken up, not even to use the bathroom, after she left.

She unlocked the door, opened it quietly, and shut it just as soundless. When she turned around, the lamp on the stand next to the couch flipped on.

"Where the hell did you go?"

He hadn't been awake long otherwise he would've called her. Though, her phone had been in her purse, and she wouldn't have heard it ring in the loud bar. Nor had she checked it when she left. Maybe he had.

"To Frost's Pub and Grill."

"And why the hell would you go without me?"

"You were snoring like a grizzly bear. Excuse me for not wanting to mess with that."

She stalked past the couch, but he followed her to the bathroom and slapped a hand to the door before she could close it.

"Noel, it's not safe here. Or did you forget that Beth was murdered here?"

No, she hadn't forgotten.

But she refused to be afraid.

"Nick, I'm tired. I can't do this with you right now. Yell at me tomorrow." Then she knocked his arm away and slammed the door before he could try to block it again. She locked it for extra measure.

She loved her brother, but he could be so overprotective and overwhelming at times.

And she wasn't ready to forget the erotic night she had. It would be the only good thing that happened in this town.

4

He felt good.

No.

He felt great.

Amazing, spontaneous sex would do that to any person. It had been a first for Duke. Having sex in public. He wasn't sure if Anton believed his lie, but he would never admit to what he had done. He didn't think Noel would spread the word about their activities either.

Maybe his after-sex glow was still shining brightly because quite a few people mentioned how he looked different but couldn't put their finger on why.

Sex!

That's why.

While he hadn't been a monk, he was very selective on who he dated, especially with the women who lived in town. Not to mention, he went on a few dates before even jumping into bed with a woman.

The harvest festival was going off without a hitch. Duke wasn't on duty this weekend, but he still showed up to the festival when it opened at nine. Seeing crowds like they were was a beautiful sight. He hoped it stayed that way all through the holidays. They needed things to keep going forward in the right direction. Once January hit, that would be the real test to how well their town had pulled out of the horrible direction it had taken.

If only he could solve Beth's murder, he'd feel better about everything.

"Hey," Griffin said in greeting, clapping him on the back, "you're here bright and early."

"I had to see how well this would be received. I am not surprised in the least Lila has done it again."

They had fall events in the past, but nothing to this extreme. They had advertised it as the First Harvest Festival. Lila had gone all out on the festivities: hayrides, corn maze, pumpkin patch, scarecrow building contest, and live music throughout the whole weekend. Duke was glad it wasn't Aster's band in town again. It was wrong of him, but he disliked the guy. Because he'd slept with Juliet. Something Duke had never had the opportunity to do.

Because he never had the guts to ask her out. His fault, he knew that. It didn't matter though. He disliked the guy.

"She's a miracle worker." Griffin took a sip from the cup in his hand. Duke couldn't see what was inside due to a lid on it, but he figured it was hot apple cider. He had to get himself one. "I heard you met our newest neighbors, the Lancasters."

Duke nodded. "Noel and Nick. I saw Noel last night at the bar. Her brother wasn't with her. I know Eve is concerned about things not being great between them. Noel didn't mention any problems with her brother."

Of course, he hadn't asked her either. He'd had mind-blowing sex instead. He'd never had to lie to his best friend

—and boss. He hoped like hell Griffin couldn't see any mistruths in his eyes.

"Oh, they're brother and sister. Good to know. I haven't introduced myself to them yet, but I plan to. I left early to help set up here. Eve said when she left a little bit ago she heard hollering again."

Damn. He'd have to chat with Noel. If her brother was abusing her, he wouldn't stand by and let it happen. Of course, that had nothing to do with the fact he slept with her. He would've protected her either way.

"I'll talk with her."

Griffin frowned. "If you want. Or I can. She is my neighbor now."

Duke shrugged. "Yeah, sure." The last thing he wanted to do was give the impression he liked Noel a little too much.

That he wanted a repeat performance with her.

Rumors spread like wildfire in town. One peep from someone that he had a thing for a tourist, he'd never hear the end of it. That would also be a first for him. He never hooked up with people passing through town on vacation.

"Hey, I need to make the rounds. Have fun. It's your weekend off."

He waved to Griffin, deciding he needed a hot apple cider. The first sip went down too fast, burning his tongue and throat. That's how Bryce found him, wincing and making painful faces.

"I did the same thing, man. It's so good though, isn't it?" Bryce said with a chuckle.

"Delicious. The Thompson's always make good apple cider."

When possible, they always tried to supply local food and drinks. The Thompson's always supplied the apple cider during fall events because they had the best apple farm in the area.

"How's Lila?" Duke hadn't seen her yet, though he knew she was bouncing around here and would until it shut down.

"Putting out fires and making sure everyone is having a great time. Same thing she always does at these events. I'm surprised you're not working."

"I'm on shift next weekend for the parade. I offered to work, but Griffin shot me down."

No doubt from the fact he was always the first to pick up extra shifts. As Griffin had put it, take a break. Relax for once. Duke didn't know how to do that. When he was idle, his thoughts took over, and he hated when that happened. He either focused on Beth's case or how he lost his chance with Juliet. Neither subject lifted his spirits. But when he worked, he didn't have time to dwell on either one. Well, he dwelled a little on Beth's case because that was work related.

"It's a good thing. Have fun. You work too hard."

Then Bryce was off to do his mayorly duties, saying hello and schmoozing the crowd.

Duke decided to do the same thing, walk around and chat with people. When he saw her, his heart skipped a beat. He couldn't remember the last time his body reacted that way with a woman—and it wasn't Juliet.

Maybe he was moving on from the woman that would never be. He wasn't saying Noel was *the one* or anything. But a fling wouldn't hurt. It would put him in the right direction to get over Juliet. Focus his attention elsewhere.

Noel looked warm and cozy in an over-large gray sweatshirt with a college logo on it, the place he assumed she attended, and a pair of jeans that he knew showcased her beautiful ass. Of course, he couldn't see it because of the sweatshirt.

He wasn't sure if Griffin had seen her yet, but he wasn't going to miss this opportunity to talk to her. Especially when he didn't see her brother. He might've given the impression to Griffin he'd back off, but he couldn't. Not when the opportunity was right in his face.

Duke grabbed another hot apple cider and headed her way.

The smile that lit up her face made his heart rate speed up. When was the last time a woman looked at him like that? A smile just for him? It'd been so long, he couldn't remember.

"Good morning."

He wasn't sure if their next interaction would be awkward or not. They hadn't left with things uncomfortable, considering they had another beer after the supply closet visit. But he just didn't know. He was glad to realize it felt normal.

"Morning." He held out the cup. "I hope you like hot apple cider. If not, you will now be a fan. It is the best hot apple cider you will ever have."

She took the cup. "Is that right? You'd swear on a bible?"

He crossed his heart as if imprinting it in stone. "I swear."

The sweet smile she sent him made his cock twitch.

Down, boy. Not in public.

Her gorgeous hazel eyes twinkled with delight.

As much as he wanted to find a quiet space and do what they did last night, it would not be possible here. He didn't want to get arrested for indecent exposure.

Then she took a sip. Her eyes closed and a breathy sigh escaped. "You are not wrong."

"One of my favorite things to hear from a woman."

She waggled her finger. "You're trying to charm me again. Naughty."

Oh, yes, he wanted to be naughty with her. Over and over.

"I see you're alone again." He'd love to keep flirting with her, but he also needed to chat with her about her brother.

"Oh, no. Nick's here. He's…" She waved her hand toward the right, then shifted it toward the left. "Somewhere around here."

Her smile had died, and so had the mood. Way too abruptly. That would help segue him into the conversation he didn't want to have.

"Everything okay between you two?"

She pinned him with a blank stare. "Why do you ask?"

This was where he needed to tread carefully.

"Can I speak freely?"

She half-crossed her arms since she was holding the cup, eyeing him warily. He hated the look and preferred it when they were smiling and flirting. But if she was in trouble, he wanted to help her.

"Of course. I prefer honesty above all else."

So did he.

"Eve heard yelling yesterday before you two ventured to town. She mentioned she heard more this morning. I also happened to witness you two sitting in the car before you walked into the cafe and he grabbed your arm. If your brother is abusing you, I can help."

She staggered back. If the cup hadn't had a lid on it, she would've scalded her skin from the spillage. Well, it would've hit her sweatshirt, but still. It was damn hot liquid. "You think my brother is abusing me? Based on a few little arguments?" The glare on her face said he wouldn't be flirting with her again.

Shit!

"And the way he grabbed you." He was mucking this up, and Griffin wouldn't be happy when he found out, especially when he wanted to handle it. "Look, it's no secret around town what Eve went through. Since you're not from around here, I'll tell you. Her brother abused her, emotionally and physically. He even tried to kill her and he's on trial for it. So, when Eve has concerns, I listen to them. I follow through because I never want someone else to go through what she had to go through."

The ire she had fizzled. "I'm so sorry to hear all that. I can't imagine what she went through. My brother and I can get loud with each other. But that's it. He's never hurt me, nor would he ever. I appreciate you looking out for me, but I promise you nothing is wrong between us."

Then what were they arguing about? He didn't think if he asked, she'd tell him. She said she preferred honesty, so he had to take her at her word.

"If something would happen, will you promise to come to me?"

She stared at him for the longest time. "You'll be the first to know."

He noticed she didn't say she promised, but he'd take it.

"Now, Officer Fisk." She slid her arm through his. "Show me the next best thing here. Because if your knowledge about the cider is anything, then you know the rest. And I trust you."

He took her words as a deeper meaning. That she simply trusted him. The fact they could have such a serious conversation, with her on the verge of hating him, then switch right out of the awkwardness was amazing. He was grateful for it. And that it hadn't ruined things between them.

"Prepare to have the most fun you've ever had."

Her answering laughter made his cock twitch again.

He was going to have the most uncomfortable day ever.

SHE KEPT her eyes and ears out for her brother, but overall, she didn't worry too much where he was at. They had decided—after a brief argument, which the neighbors heard —they would split up at the festival. They'd cover more ground in their investigation.

Not that it was much of an investigation. They were being subtle about the questions they asked or the comments they made. They didn't want to spook anyone or give the impression they knew Beth. At least, not until the killer was out in the open.

Nick, of course, wanted to stick together. He worried about her, which wasn't necessary. She could handle herself. After having a lively conversation about the matter, he conceded and said they could split up.

She was loving that decision right now.

Hanging out with Duke had been unexpected, but something she was enjoying. He knew everyone in town. He knew which people were tourists, and which ones were residents. That helped her figure out who she should focus on for further inquiries. At a later date, of course. She couldn't do much with Duke by her side.

He would be a wealth of information himself. He worked for the police. Not that she could come right out and ask about Beth's case. Then she'd be the one interrogated, not the other way around.

Her brother had skills. A talent that could get him in trouble if he ever made the wrong move. Being good with a computer had helped them immensely. He was able to hack into the police database before they left for Sleighville and get every piece of information on Beth's case.

It wasn't that helpful.

Because the police didn't have much. No evidence. No suspect. They hadn't even known she'd disappeared. Based on the statements they read, they had thought Beth left town without telling anyone. They'd been proven wrong when her body had been fished out of Tinsel Lake.

She had nothing to point to a resident being the killer, but her gut said a tourist didn't do this. Someone from town did. Because her rental place had been cleared of her stuff, making it appear as if she left town. How would a tourist know where she lived? Well, maybe they followed her. It wasn't much to go on, but her instincts said she was dealing with someone familiar with the area.

That meant she needed to make herself familiar with the area and all the people in it.

Today, hanging off Duke's arm, put her right in the middle of it. She'd met so many people, she knew she wouldn't remember all their names. But she wouldn't forget their faces.

The day was going by too fast.

Duke peered at her from his side of the table as he jotted on a piece of paper. She met his gaze, smirking, writing on her own.

"Which one did you pick?" he asked, putting his piece of paper in the slit in the wooden box.

"You first."

She'd never participated in a scarecrow contest. Voting

on the best one created. And one where they were all Christmas themed. It was funny thinking about it.

"The snowman one. By far, the best."

She cocked a brow. "Ummm...I don't know about that. I mean, the snowman was creative, but the one who looked like Rudolph was a masterpiece. The detail with the horns alone was amazing."

"Antlers. Not horns." He chuckled, then rubbed his chin, pondering that. "You have a point."

Ugh. Okay, so she didn't know her reindeers. Whatever. "Yeah, I do. You should dig yours out."

"But the fact they made all the hay white, like, snowy white, is impressive. Hands down, makes it the best one."

"I guess we'll see who's right." She looped her arm through his again.

She'd done that a lot throughout the day. He never protested, so why stop? She liked touching him. Hearing the sharp intake of breath at times from him. The sultry glances he sent her way. The slight bulge she would see form in the front of his pants. He liked her holding onto him as much as she enjoyed it.

"Yo, sis!"

She looked over her shoulder to see Nick waving at her and heading her way. They turned around, and despite not wanting to, she let go of Duke's arm. She didn't need to hear crap from Nick on how she was latching onto the officer. She'd hear it anyway.

"I have been looking everywhere for you."

"Did you forget to put your contacts in this morning?" she jested.

He rolled his eyes. "Har, har. Where have you been?"

Translated into, did she leave the area without telling him? No. Why would she?

"Enjoying the festivities." Then she brushed Duke's arm. "With Officer Fisk."

Nick looked at him. "I can take her off your hands if she's being clingy. She can get like that."

She would kill her brother when they got back to the cottage.

"We're having a great time. I hope you're enjoying the festival," Duke said smoothly as if her brother didn't embarrass her.

"Oh, yeah. This is loads of fun. Never been to a place that had so much Christmas cheer mixed with fall-like themes."

"That is the purpose of the town." Nick glanced at her, not amused. "By the way, you should stop yelling at me for silly things. Officer Fisk here thinks you're abusing me."

Nick's mouth dropped open. "You're joking, right?"

"Eve, your neighbor, has heard quite a bit of yelling coming from the cottage." Duke's stance went straighter as if he were gearing up for a fight. "I also saw you grab her arm."

"I would never."

Duke continued as if her brother never spoke. "Noel assures me that you're not abusing her, and I'm taking her word for it. But one wrong move, and I will arrest you."

Nick stared at him with his mouth wide open for a few seconds before bursting out with laughter. Duke's entire body went rigid. Noel wanted to smack her brother. Of course, she was the one who brought it up.

"You do realize my sister could drop kick my ass without blinking, right? She has before. It hurts like hell. If anyone's abusing anyone, she's your suspect."

Yep. She would beat his ass when they got back.

Duke didn't look amused.

"No, seriously. She knows how to fight. Even if I wanted

to hurt her, which I don't, maybe I'd get lucky with one punch before she took me down."

Duke's stance slackened, then he looked at her. She offered a gentle grin. "I mean, I know a few defensive moves."

"Ha! She's an expert at kick boxing. Trust me."

"Okay, well, then." Duke matched her gentle smile, but she also saw the seriousness behind it. "Don't make me arrest you either."

She wouldn't mind him putting handcuffs on her. Then having his dirty way with her. "Of course not."

"Hey, there you are."

Noel didn't recognize the gentleman approaching them. They'd met a lot of people today, but not everyone. The uniform said he worked with Duke.

"Problem?" Duke asked.

"No, no, been busy with a few issues, but nothing serious. Eve was looking for you."

"Where is she? I can go to her."

The man shrugged, laughing. "Bouncing around this place as much as Lila is. I'm not sure." The man then looked at her and Nick before holding out his hand to Nick. "I'm Chief Griffin Stuart. You're renting the cottage next door to me."

Well, that was interesting. They were right next to the chief of police. Noel couldn't decide if that was a good or bad thing.

"Nick Lancaster." Her brother tossed a lazy hand toward her after shaking Griffin's hand. "My sister Noel."

Griffin shook her hand. "Welcome to Sleighville. I hope you're enjoying your visit. I apologize you have to share such a tiny cottage."

"Oh, it's no problem. We booked at the last minute, and

it was all that was left. My brother is used to sleeping on the couch."

"Ouch, Noel. That wounds me."

Paybacks were a bitch. He threw her under the bus earlier, she was returning the favor. "His wife wears the pants in the family. So he's delegated to the couch more often than not."

Nick crossed his arms, the irritation rising in his features. "Or I choose to sleep there to get away from her."

The chief of police and Duke kept glancing from her to her brother.

"I guess that means you're married to Eve. Please tell her I'm sorry she's heard our arguing. He won't admit it, but he does get cranky when he doesn't get a full ten hours of sleep. And well, he's sleeping on the couch, so..."

"And she hogged all the damn hot water this morning. Do you know how unpleasant it is to take a cold shower?"

Griffin frowned. "The hot water heater should hold a good amount. I should check it out if it ran out."

"Chief," Nick said with a serious tone, "my sister wastes water and takes the longest showers on the planet. It's horrible for the planet. Half the time she doesn't recycle either."

At that, she couldn't hold in her laughter. "You're ridiculous. Like you recycle!" She was still chuckling when she looked at Griffin. "Ignore my stupid brother. I'm sorry that we upset Eve. Duke already talked to me about it, and his concerns. Her concerns. I promise you, my brother would never hurt me."

"Again, I would never be able to because you would kick my ass."

Griffin's guarded expression evaporated and he produced a smile. "I'm glad to hear that. I apologize if we stepped into your business, but my wife likes to look out for other people. Of course, as do I."

"As she should."

"We would love to have you over for supper. I don't know how long you two are in town, but if you're still here on Monday, we'd love to have you over."

Wow. Surprising to get a dinner invite from the chief of police. But hell yeah! This was the kind of in they needed.

"Thank you. Umm...we'd like that." She looked at Nick, who nodded. "We're not sure how long we'll be in town. We've...ah...kind of taken an extended leave of absence. We needed to get away after a death in the family."

She hated lying, especially to Duke, but they couldn't tell anyone their real reason for being in town.

Duke's hand brushed hers, yet he didn't grab a hold of it. "I'm so sorry to hear that. Who did you lose?"

"Our sister." They held a long stare, before she broke contact first, smiling, maybe a little too brightly at Griffin. "What time should we be there?"

"Six o'clock." The chief of police glanced at Duke. "Why don't you come over too, Duke? You missed game night last night. This can make up for it."

"Yeah, sure."

Then Griffin bid his goodbye and left. Not long after, Duke also parted ways with her. She missed his presence the moment he walked away. She and Nick left shortly afterward.

"Do you think we threw them off with our ridiculous banter?" Nick asked as he drove back to the cottage.

"That you abuse me?"

"Har, har. We both know you can kick my ass."

She crossed her arms, staring out the window. "Then

why do we keep arguing about the fact you don't want me going anywhere alone? I can protect myself."

Nick pulled into the driveway, shutting off the car. "Did you forget Beth used to go to the kickboxing classes with you? She could hold her own too. And look what happened."

She trailed her gaze from the window to him, loosening her arms.

"I'm not so sure about this dinner with the chief of police and an officer," Nick said. "I don't want them asking questions we're not willing to answer. We should keep our distance."

Oh, she was definitely not confessing she had sex with Duke.

"Or getting closer could get us answers."

"We've looked over all the information on the case. They have jack shit. For all we know, one of them killed her."

"They were both ready to arrest you for hurting me. I doubt it."

"Well, we attracted too much attention getting a little too loud with each other. No more of that."

"Yeah, I agree. So stop telling me what to do and we won't have a problem." With that, she exited the car.

She felt her brother fuming behind her, wanting to let loose his ire.

He was right, of course. They attracted too much attention. The plan had been to come in under the radar, poke around, and find the person who killed their sister.

5

HE RUSHED through changing out of his uniform, hopping in the shower, and dressing. When he stared at himself in the mirror, he knew he was trying too hard. He never dressed up when going over to Griffin's. Not even to impress Juliet.

Another ding against him when it came to his feelings for her.

Yet, here he was, putting on a nice sweater and gray slacks to impress Noel.

He threw off the clothes, letting them gather in a rumpled pile on the floor, and put on a pair of jeans with a blue T-shirt. There. Much better. Like he usually dressed when he went over to one of the Stuarts' places.

He didn't want to tip anyone off he had a thing for Noel. And he already blew that when he hung around her the entire day on Saturday. Though, over the course of his shift today, no one had mentioned it. No one had given him crap.

So he wasn't about to start it now by dressing abnormally.

He pulled into Griffin's driveway, wiping his palms on his

pants before getting out of the truck. He pressed a light kiss to Eve's cheek when she opened the door and waited in the foyer while she shut it. Walter, their old soul cat, strolled into the area, brushing his leg in greeting, and then sauntered back out of the area.

"Hey, I found the contact information for that guy I know. Custom made. A little more pricier than you want, but Griffin will love it," Duke whispered.

This had been the reason Eve had been looking for him on Saturday. The real Christmas holiday was around the corner, and Eve was doing her Christmas shopping. She wanted to get Griffin a new fishing pole, but not just any kind. She wanted it specially made for him. He knew a guy that custom made poles with anything a person wanted. Character-themed. Movie-themed. Favorite colors. You asked for it, the dude would do it.

"You know money's not an issue."

He forgot sometimes that Eve owned a hotel chain, and she was insanely rich. Because she didn't act like it. She was working with her board of directors to create small cottages around Sleighville. They wanted a hotel. They were at a stalemate because neither would give in. Eve was right. A hotel wouldn't fit in their town. The cottages were more the town's style. The war on the issue had been going on for almost a year. Neither one would cave. And he knew Eve never would, so they were waiting for the board to see things her way.

"I gave him your number. He'll call you tomorrow for more specifics about what you want."

Eve touched his shoulder. "You're a lifesaver. Griffin's so hard to buy for. I want to get him more than that and I have no clue."

"Whatever you get him, he'll love."

He followed Eve into the living room where Griffin was situated on the couch watching a re-run of yesterday's football game. Eve left for the kitchen, and he took a seat next to him.

"What were you two whispering about in the foyer?"

Duke chuckled. "It's on a need-to-know basis, and you don't need to know."

Griffin slapped his chest as if wounded. "That hurt. I'll pry it out of her later."

"Or you can leave it alone."

The way he said it must've convinced Griffin it was the wiser option.

"So I invited Bryce and Lila too, but they're crashing tonight. Bryce insisted Lila rest and relax."

After the busy weekend she had, she needed it. Plus, two weeks ago, Bryce and Lila had moved out of the cottage Nick and Noel were now renting. They had been living there since they had gotten together. Bryce had never felt comfortable moving back into the house he had shared with Denise. It sold last month. Bryce used the profit on it to buy them a new house. Duke knew they were much happier in a bigger space. So Lila had to be wiped from it all. Moving into a new place. Putting together the Harvest Festival and then being at it for every second it went on. He was glad Bryce put his foot down and made her stay home. In between all that, they were also planning their wedding for next summer. So much going on for them.

Nick and Noel were lucky they even got the cottage to rent. If they hadn't moved out, there wouldn't have been anything for them to rent.

"She deserves it."

"Definitely. I did invite Juliet."

It would've been weird if he hadn't. If one Stuart was invited, so were the rest.

"But I have a feeling you don't care about that."

Griffin had a beer in his hand, and Duke wanted one as well. "I don't follow."

"You were with Noel a long time at the festival. I've never seen you...hang out with a tourist for so long."

Well, he'd never been attracted to one as he was with her.

"She's nice. I was being friendly."

"Hey, I'm not complaining. I like seeing you focus on someone else."

"You mean you like me not pining over your sister anymore."

"Aster's not around. You could ask her out."

That opportunity had already passed him by. If Juliet wanted something to do with him, she would've given him a sign. Like Noel had. Her heated looks and beckoning smile told him he was wanted in every way from the very beginning. Juliet looked at him like nothing more than a brother.

"I'm confused, Grif. Ask out your sister, or focus on an out-of-towner? Which one?"

"Whatever one makes you happy. You've been my best friend for so long, you feel like my brother. Making it official wouldn't hurt."

Duke laughed. That was never going to happen. And it sounded like Griffin was leaning more toward he wanted Duke to focus on his sister, not an outsider.

"Yeah, I know," Griffin agreed as if Duke had spoken it out loud. "Juliet's lost right now. After her divorce...the fling with Aster. I don't know. I worry about her."

She'd hate that if she knew.

"I worry about you too."

"I'm fine, Griffin."

"You're working too much, Duke. It's not your fault you haven't solved Beth's murder."

Then why did it feel like it was his fault?

He was assigned the case. He should have more than what he had. Which was nadda. No clue to lead him in the right direction.

If only they would've dug deeper into her leaving town. Treated it as a missing person's case right away instead of what they all assumed.

But they hadn't, and dwelling on that wouldn't change anything.

"I think you should keep your distance from Noel. And Nick," he said, adding him as an afterthought.

"Why is that? You've invited them over for supper. That's not keeping your distance."

"I don't know. That interaction with them was odd. I've got a weird feeling about them. Like they're hiding something. I invited them over as an apology if we offended them with our concerns, and to find out more about them."

Hiding something. Like what? In his interactions with Noel, he never got the vibe she was holding back. Of course, he could be biased. He did sleep with her in the back of the bar. They never touched their personal lives much. They kept it light and carefree. Like flings were supposed to be. Not that he'd ever had one, but he figured that's how they operated. You didn't dig too deep into the other person's affairs.

"Just because you and your siblings don't squabble like they do, doesn't mean they're hiding something. Every family is different."

Griffin seemed to mull that over. "That is true. Still, be careful around them."

For a moment, he thought Griffin might've found out what he'd done with Noel. Yet, Griffin would also come right out and say if he did.

His best friend was looking out for him, something he'd do in return.

Juliet arrived a short time later. Griffin left the room to grab them a drink.

"So?"

Duke chuckled. "So."

"Come on. You didn't like the fact I had a thing with Aster, and now you're doing the same thing."

What had Juliet heard? And why in the hell did she care?

"I didn't think my dating life was any of your concern."

Juliet crossed her arms as she lounged on the small reclining chair. "Mine wasn't yours either and yet you made it known you didn't approve."

"I'm sorry. I never meant to step on your toes. You are free to do whatever you want."

"I know I am," she snapped. Then she sighed. "Do you have a thing going with this Noel chick, or what? I heard she was hanging off your arm at the festival all day."

And he enjoyed every moment of it.

Juliet had been manning a table for the cafe the entire event. While they stopped at the table, he hadn't spoken to her besides an amiable hello.

"I'm being friendly. She's nice."

Same words he said to Griffin, but in reverse order.

Juliet huffed.

Duke frowned. "Are you...jealous?"

"Ha! Why would I be jealous?"

"I have no idea."

"You butt in my business, I'm returning the favor."

Not fair, and she knew it. He never stepped in her way with Aster. Was he a little abrupt and cold to Aster? Sure, but he never voiced his concerns or told Juliet to stop what she was doing. Because it wasn't his place.

"I'm sorry I was short with Aster, but that's all I did. I never told you to stop what you were doing." She continued to glare at him. "Let's get it out in the open. I've had a thing for you for a long time. I was the idiot who never did anything about it. Why? I don't know. Maybe because I didn't want to lose my best friend if things didn't work out. Maybe because I thought I'd never have a chance with you. But I blew it. Aster rolled in, barely blinked, and you were in his arms. I'll admit, it pissed me off. You never looked at me that way. I've accepted that, Juliet. The only thing I've ever wanted for you is to be happy. And if that playboy makes you happy, then end of story."

She sat up and leaned forward. "I'm sorry, Duke. I knew you had a crush or whatever. I tried to picture being with you and all I could imagine was kissing one of my brothers."

Not what any man wanted to hear. To be thought of as a brother when you pined over a woman for so long.

"I know things have been weird between us lately and I hate it. I want it to stop. I want to go back to the way things were. I'm sorry I jumped down your throat. I had a bad day."

"No need to apologize. We're good. I'm always here for you, Juliet."

"That's why, one day, you're going to make one lucky woman's day. I bite your head off and you're telling me to forget about it."

"Do you want to talk about what's bugging you?"

Because he knew it wasn't just her having a bad day. She'd been acting like this for a while. He hated to say since Aster had left. She'd gone and fallen for the man when she said she wouldn't. That it wasn't just a fling. That had to be it.

She curled her feet under her legs. "I told you. I had a bad day." Then her lips twisted upward. "So now that we've established I'm not jealous. Tell me about Noel. You don't hang out with an out-of-towner all day. In fact, I can't recall a time you've ever done that."

At one time, he used to be able to tell Juliet anything. They had a very close relationship.

Ugh! Like he was one of her brothers.

He should've seen it ages ago that she'd never look at him as anything more.

But this thing with Noel—if there even was a thing—he didn't want to talk about it.

"I was—"

"Being friendly. Right. Got it." She rolled her eyes. "You don't fool me, mister."

He was afraid he might not be able to fool anyone else much longer.

"Yo, MORON, LET'S GO!" Noel hollered near the front door, checking her phone. "We're going to be late."

Nick's head appeared from the hallway. "Hold your damn horses." He pointed at her. "No more hollering. See, you instigate it all. They're going to think I'm beating you again." Then he disappeared. She heard the water running and knew he was finishing up in the bathroom.

He wasn't wrong. But he was so slow getting ready. Every. Single. Time. She hated being late.

They had a productive day yesterday, hanging around town, shopping and mingling with the townsfolk. She didn't ask any questions about Beth, but the more she interacted with people, the more they'd get comfortable with her. She was almost ready to start probing a little harder.

She needed to find out who killed her sister, but also why she left them to begin with. In the three months she had lived in Sleighville, Beth never called. Never returned her calls. It hurt. It made her wonder what the hell they had done to push her away.

Instead of venturing into town today, not wanting to seem too pushy with people, they stayed in. Noel pored over the case file. Of course, nothing new popped out at her. She didn't expect anything to either.

What she needed was a new perspective. She needed to pepper people with questions. But she couldn't do that, not without raising suspicions, but that's what she wanted to do.

Nick rounded the corner, smiling like the devil. "Let's go already. You're holding us up." Then he brushed by her, opening the door.

Sometimes she wanted to smack her brother. By the time they crossed the short distance across the lawn, they were two minutes late. Because of him!

Eve opened the door, gesturing them in. "I'm so glad you could make it. Welcome."

Noel appreciated she didn't bring up the whole abusive angle again. That issue needed to be swept under the rug and kept there.

She held out a bottle of wine, something they had picked up yesterday. "I wasn't sure if you liked red or white, but I opted for red because it's a Christmas color." She chuckled, shrugging.

"You're in luck. I love red."

Eve walked them into the living room where she introduced them to Juliet, Griffin's sister. She beamed at Duke, and while she wanted to take a seat next to him, she settled for the couch opposite his and sat by her brother.

"So you own Noel's Cafe?" her brother asked Juliet, leaning toward her. "Because I have to say the food there is off the charts. Seriously delicious."

"Thank you. It's my pride and joy. And of course, since Eve moved here, we have the best baked goods I think in the whole state."

Eve waved her off with a shy grin.

"It's true. Stop it, girl." Juliet looked back at Nick. "What do you two do? I'm sorry to hear about your sister passing. It's never easy losing a loved one."

Another conversation Noel didn't want to talk about. That would require them to lie, and she didn't want to lie to the chief of police and his family. Or Duke. Especially not him.

"Thank you. Yeah, it's been hard." Nick grabbed her knee, squeezing. She knew not in a comforting way. More like warning her to maintain her composure and not fail in her acting skills. She had a tendency to get nervous, and a little beat red when she had to lie. It was a good thing she had been wearing an oversize sweatshirt on Saturday when the topic came up. It hid the redness that had spread on her chest. Tonight she had on a nice cashmere V-neck sweater that would display the redness like a neon blinking light.

"But to answer your first question, I work as a mechanic. I'm good with cars. Love working under a hood."

She wanted to snicker at that. He was a mechanic. And yes, he was good with cars. But he loved working under a hood...of a computer. Well, if computers had hoods. That was his real talent. Not that he'd ever confess that.

"And my sister works as a bartender. She makes a mean martini."

Compared to this group of people—a chief of police, an officer, an owner of a café—she fell short in many, many ways.

"I love me a good martini," Juliet replied, swiping her tongue across her upper lip. "Maybe we can convince you to make us ladies one later."

"Hey, what about us men?" Griffin asked, as if offended, though she heard the teasing tone in his voice.

"Well, I don't know Nick's preference, but I've never seen you or Duke drink anything but beer. Maybe a glass of whiskey or something, but a martini? Seriously?"

"I'm saying you don't have to exclude us. I might want to try one."

"Well, you can't. More for me." Juliet threw Nick a pretty smile. "None for you either, even if you like them. Girls only."

"And more for you," Nick replied smoothly.

Eww!

If she didn't know any better, Juliet was flirting with her brother, and he was doing it right back. Did he forget he was married? To a bitch, but still.

Juliet drew forward, closer to Nick. "And where are you from?"

"The big Apple. Bright lights, controlled chaos, and in a city that never sleeps."

"I've always wanted to go to New York. Tell me more."

She let Nick have that conversation, tuning him out. She didn't want to see him flirting with someone.

After about five minutes, she excused herself to use the bathroom. Eve was in the hallway when she stepped out. Either waiting for her, or perfect timing.

"I have a few ingredients available if you want to try

making a martini of some kind. Juliet asked again when you left."

"Yeah, sure."

She had a great memory when it came to certain things. Alcoholic drinks were one of them. Depending on the items she had, Noel could make just about anything. They had a lot to choose from.

After eyeing it all, she went with a White Christmas Martini. A little bit of vodka, white chocolate liqueur, creme de cacao, and half-and-half, and you got pure perfection. Christmas in a glass.

Eve's first sip elicited a soft moan. "This is delicious. I've been told I have magic in my hands when I bake. You have magic in your hands making drinks. I swear I don't even taste the alcohol."

"And that's what makes it dangerous." Noel took her own sip, enjoying the smooth, robust flavor.

"I need to deliver this asap."

"I'll clean up and be right out there."

Eve waved her off, but Noel insisted. She didn't like leaving messes behind. She put the bottles back where they came from, wiped up the counter even though she hadn't spilled one thing, and then turned around with her drink in her hand.

Duke stood close. A little too close where she was surprised she hadn't heard him approach.

"Juliet and Eve won't share. I'm hoping you'll be different."

She lifted her drink, sipping with a sly smirk. "Do I get anything in return for sharing?"

"What would you like?"

A lot of things, especially from this man.

His hands on her. His lips in places where it'd be indecent. His cock—

She shouldn't let her mind wander into such dangerous territory. But Duke must've read her expression because he moved in closer, giving her no space to escape, his body trapping her between him and the counter.

Then he brushed his lips with hers and she needed no further coaxing to give in. She opened her mouth, letting his tongue dive in.

She moaned at the contact, and he shooshed her against her lips.

Right. Of course. They were in a house with other people and anyone could walk in at any time. But that knowledge didn't stop the kiss.

He pushed into her, igniting her senses even more. His cock was hard and aching and wanting to play even closer to her. She wished like hell she could accommodate his desire.

When she moaned again, Duke broke the kiss, pressing a finger to her lips.

"You moan too loud." He bit his bottom lip. "I like it, but not here."

Which meant somewhere else then?

Yes, please.

"So about that taste?"

Of her? She was game.

But then she realized he meant the martini in her hand. She held it out.

"One small taste. And no telling the ladies I caved."

"It's our little secret." Then he gulped instead of sipped. "And I need more than a small taste."

He handed the glass back to her and walked out of the kitchen.

Damn! That man was going to be big trouble for her.

6

HE HADN'T LIKED it when they sat across from each other in the living room. So when supper was ready, he made sure to get a spot next to Noel. Juliet was across from him and smirked the moment he planted his butt in the chair.

Okay, yeah. So he liked Noel. Maybe he was being a little too obvious about it, but so what? He was a grown man who could make his own decisions. She'd done the same thing when Aster was in town. Though by her wicked expression, she found it amusing, and not that he was making a bad decision.

Conversation flowed well. Nick and Noel fit into their group as if they'd always been in it. Duke was bummed Bryce and Lila had missed this. They would've enjoyed the evening as well.

Eve made pumpkin pie for dessert, and like all the things she baked, it was delicious. And he wasn't even a big fan of pumpkin anything.

They congregated back in the living room, and he managed to get a seat by Noel again. Another damn smirk from Juliet. Before they had sat down, Noel had made the ladies another martini. While it wasn't his kind of drink, he wanted another taste. If only to get another taste of her. The kiss in the kitchen hadn't been long enough.

Except Duke didn't know how to ask her out. She was on vacation. For such a horrible reason too. Having to get away because of a death in the family was devastating. They must've been close to their sister. He felt for her. For Nick.

While he wanted to get to know her more, he knew she wasn't staying here permanently. But there was no harm in having sex again. A casual fling. If they were both on board knowing what it was. He figured since they'd already had sex, then they were both on the same page for what was happening between them.

But he felt weird asking her out. To have sex.

Not to mention, he didn't want her brother finding out. The man may seem easygoing, but there was a rough edge to him that had Duke keeping an eye on him at all times. He believed Noel when she said her brother didn't touch her, but it never hurt to stay vigilant.

"This was nice. You two have to stop into the cafe before you leave town," Juliet said, finishing off her martini. "I know you said you didn't know how long you're staying, so what else do you plan to do around here? You should stay for the Halloween parade. It's our first one we've ever had and it's going to be amazing."

Nick, who sat on the couch opposite his sister, shared a look with her before responding. "I think we're staying for the parade. I loved the Christmas touch at the festival, so I can't wait to see what the parade offers."

"You're going to see Santa dressed up in a costume," Griffin said with a laugh.

"How will that work?" Nick asked.

Duke couldn't wait to see how that worked as well. It was hilarious thinking about it.

"He'll have his white hair and beard with his signature red hat." Griffin grinned. "But you have to see the parade to see what he's being for Halloween."

Nick slapped his knee with a boisterous laugh. "I can't wait."

"I want to do some more shopping. I know I've been in the stores a few times already, but I'm a careful shopper. I don't buy something the first time, and there are a few things I thought about and decided I now to have them," Noel said, taking a sip of her martini, which was almost gone. "But tomorrow Nick and I were going to try some fishing at Tinsel Lake."

Duke tensed, his mind conjuring the brutal image of Beth. The problem was he was sitting by Noel who sensed his tension.

She looked at him. "Is that a bad lake to go to?"

He forced out a smile, hoping she couldn't tell how fake it was. "No, of course not. Tinsel Lake is the best around town. You can catch some nice sunnies there."

"Oh, okay."

He swallowed hard. "Your brother is going with you?"

He had to make sure he heard correctly because he would not allow Noel to go alone. Not after finding Beth's body there. Not when he hadn't located her killer yet. He didn't care if she thought that possessive or not his business, but he was making it his business. She'd have to deal with it.

"Yeah, she's dragging me along," Nick groaned.

"Good. You should go midmorning, early afternoon. The fish bite better then."

Noel flashed him a brilliant smile. "Thanks for the tip."

It wasn't a lie. But it also made him feel better to know

they wouldn't be there super early in the morning or late at night.

He doubted Beth was killed at the lake, only her body had been dumped there. But on the off-chance his gut was wrong, he didn't want Noel there at a time where someone could sneak up on them.

From there, the conversation ended and Juliet was the first to leave. Followed by Nick and Noel. Duke had no chance to see if she wanted to go for drinks later—then sex —without asking her brother along as well. He wanted it to be a party of two.

Eve said goodbye then left the room, leaving him alone with Griffin.

"You wanted to tell them about Beth, didn't you?"

"As long as her brother goes along with her, it should be fine. But I don't like the thought of her going alone."

Griffin nodded. "I thought we decided the killer dumped her body there."

"Yeah, we did. Doesn't mean I like the thought of her there alone."

Griffin's eyes narrowed. Not in a stern way, but more concerned than anything. "Do you have a thing for Noel? I thought it was odd you hung around her all day on Saturday."

"I was being friendly."

But the look Griffin gave him said he didn't believe that excuse any more than Juliet had.

"Drive safe."

He was grateful Griffin decided to leave it at that. It was one thing to have a short fling, it was another thing to announce it to everyone he knew.

Duke left and drove home. The first thing he did when he unlocked his door was go to his spare room. Flicking the light switch on, the bright glare jolted him. Then the brutal image of Beth jolted him some more.

Such a young woman to have lost her life so soon.

He fell asleep at his desk, looking over the case files for the billionth time, not waking up until seven in the morning. It was a damn good thing he had today off, otherwise he would've been late to work. But since he was working the weekend, he had today and tomorrow off so he wasn't working more than five days in a row. Griffin was always great about giving his officers the appropriate time off.

His body ached from sleeping all night long in a terrible position, so he worked out, lifting weights, running on the treadmill, and doing some stretches in his basement. Then he showered, made coffee, and had something to eat. After all that, he felt more like himself and ready to tackle the day.

It was eleven o'clock when he checked the microwave for the time. Not too early, but not too late.

Did Noel and Nick follow his advice? Because if so, now would be around the time they would head to the lake. Since he never asked for Noel's number at any point in their interactions, he had no way of finding out.

Unless he drove to the lake.

It couldn't hurt to check on her. Make sure they knew the right spots to fish, where they'd catch the most. He forgot to mention that last night.

Yeah.

That wouldn't hurt at all.

It had nothing to do with the anxiety coursing through his veins thinking of Noel near the body of water that had coughed up a dead body.

Nothing at all.

THEY STOOD at the end of the dock, the morning air chilling her to the bone. She'd worn a pair of sweatpants, first to keep her warm, and second because she didn't care if they got dirty from fishing. If one got dirty from fishing. She had no idea as this was her first time. She'd also worn an oversized black sweater, yet neither item was keeping her very warm. The cool breeze made her shiver every time it hit her, which was every other second. It was a very windy day.

They'd gotten to the lake a little after ten. They had been in luck. No one else was there. So they headed for the location mentioned in the report where Beth's body had been pulled out. Of course, being how many months later, nothing looked out of place. No clues popped out at them. Noel hadn't expected anything to pop out at them. But she needed to see where her sister had been dumped like she was a piece of trash.

After poking around the area for quite a long time, they decided, in case anyone else showed up, they should fish. Like they had said they were going to do last night. No need to draw suspicion on themselves for a tiny lie. So they made it reality.

She managed to put a worm on her line and cast it into the water while her brother struggled with even getting the line to release on the rod.

"Fishing is the dumbest sport on the planet," he grumbled as his fingers messed with the line. "If it's even considered a sport. I don't think it should be."

Noel snickered, then sat down, dangling her legs over the side of the dock. "Need some help?"

"No!"

She heard stomping going on. Then more cursing. Another round of stomping. Followed by more cursing.

If she didn't help him untangle the mess he had created, she'd be ready to leave by the time he accomplished that.

"Ugh!" Then he threw the pole in the water. They watched it sink below the murky surface, except for the bobber attached to the line.

"I paid good money for that fishing pole. You will be getting that out of the water."

"I wouldn't call forty bucks good money. I bet that's cheap compared to what the pros pay."

She glared at her brother. "Then give me forty bucks."

"Fine." He plopped down on his belly, reaching for the bobber. It was just out of his reach.

"If forty bucks is so cheap, hand it over. Why are you trying to retrieve it?"

"Hey, Noel," Nick said, tossing a disgusted look over his shoulder. "Shut up."

Then he scooted forward some, wiggling his fingers, nearly touching the bobber. So he moved forward a bit more, almost snagging the bobber in the next try. But the splash from his hand moved the bobber away a bit, causing Nick to scoot forward a bit more. By this point, his whole chest was hanging off the dock, and Noel couldn't stop the evil smirk from spreading across her lips. How long would he be able to hold himself on the dock?

It turned out, not much longer. His hand that had been trying to anchor him to the dock, lost its grip and Nick tumbled headfirst into the lake.

Her laughter rang around the area, and she was still laughing when Nick resurfaced.

"You think this is funny?" He swam toward her as if to grab her feet and pull her in with him, but she was faster, scrambling to her feet.

"Don't forget the pole while you're in there."

Nick tossed an armful of water her way before going for the fishing pole. While she managed to get out of the way for most of it, some water did hit her sweats. With the cool breeze already causing her to shiver, that wasn't going to help her.

Maybe it was time to leave.

Nick climbed back onto the dock, tossing the mangled fishing pole onto the wooden planks. "Happy now?"

"Very. Thank you."

"It's not like we're ever going fishing again in our lives."

"True, but I wouldn't have gotten such good entertainment otherwise."

"I hate you sometimes."

She blew him a kiss, offering a dose of love in return. Nick would never hate her. That was his way of expressing his love.

At the sound of tires crunching on the ground, she turned around. Another smile, this one full of bliss, erupted on her face when Duke got out of the truck.

"What's he doing here?" Nick muttered.

When he pulled his own fishing gear out, that answered Nick's question.

"I hope you don't mind I join you," Duke said as he walked toward them, his boots clomping on the wooden planks. Duke eyed her brother, unable to hide his grin. "A big catch give you problems?"

"Yeah, something like that." Then Nick's lips widened with happiness. "Since you plan on fishing, how about you stay with Noel and give her a ride home? I think I'm fished out for the day."

The day had turned around in her favor. Time alone with Duke. Hell yeah.

"No problem. You should get out of those wet clothes too. Don't want to catch a cold or something."

"Thanks, man." Nick grabbed his mangled pole and clapped Duke on the back, strolling by him. Without turning around, Nick hollered, "Bring me supper tonight, sis. I'm counting on you."

Loser! She wasn't going to share any of her fish with him. Not if she had to do all the work.

"Do I want to know what happened?" Duke asked when they were alone.

"Oh, I'd love to tell you the story. It's a great one."

He tossed his head for her to follow. "Tell me on the way. I know a better spot where we'll catch your brother a good meal for tonight."

She reeled in her line, grabbed her belongings, and walked with Duke around the lake. The exact opposite side where Beth's body had been found.

They sat down and started getting their rods ready. Duke's muffled laughter had her pausing in putting on a worm.

"What?"

"I'm going to take a guess that you and your brother— big city folks that you are—have never fished in your life."

A lopsided smile touched her lips. "What gave us away?"

"Your brother dripping wet for one. His tangled pole for another." Duke pointed at the teeny tiny portion of the worm she attached. "You need to put more of the worm on. No fish is going to bite what you have."

"Yeah, but it wiggles and..." She made a disgusted face, sticking out her tongue.

"Give me your hook."

She obliged, happy to have Duke by her side, not just because he was putting the bait on the hook. She enjoyed spending time with him. And if the place continued to remain empty, another round of sex with him wouldn't hurt.

He dropped the hook when he finished, meeting her sultry gaze. Her eyes must've told him what her mind had been salivating about. He leaned over, cupping her cheek, and kissed her.

A sweet, slow kiss that said he wasn't in a rush to leave her side any more than she was to leave his.

The kiss ended way too soon.

"We better fish before this escalates to something more."

She bit her lip, teasing him with a come-hither smile. "I'm not opposed to something more."

This time he wrapped his hand around the back of her head, pulling her closer. He deepened the kiss, eliciting a low moan from her.

"God, I love it when you moan like that," he said in between the twisting of their lips.

His hand tangled in her hair while his other found her waist. She knew they were about to get it on, and she hoped like hell he was carrying another condom in his wallet.

Then the slam of a door had them breaking away, their heavy breathing the only sounds by them.

She glanced to see a family of four take a spot on the dock.

"I guess we're fishing," he said, picking his rod up.

She retrieved hers as well, casting her line. "For now."

The pleasure in his eyes when he turned toward her had her insides warming to the point where she wanted to take off her sweater. She was no longer cold. Not with Duke by her side.

7

————

Duke glanced at his watch, shocked to see it was already three o'clock. Time had flown by. They fished the entire time. A few other people had come and gone while they were there. But they had been tucked in their own little corner that no one bothered them. No one was close enough to see them steal a kiss or two in-between catching a boat-load of fish. They both caught their limit. Nick would be getting his fish fry tonight.

Noel was lucky he had come. She hadn't even brought a bucket or a cooler for any of the potential fish she would've caught. He had. Not to mention, when she did catch one, he had to take it off the hook. She squealed and groaned every time she tried to touch one, insisting he do it. He was more than happy to do anything for her. Not just to get in her pants. Because he enjoyed doing it. He enjoyed her company.

The afternoon had been filled with fun and laughter, something he hadn't done in a long time. At least, not with a woman he found attractive.

By the time they walked to his truck and loaded it all up,

the place was deserted. He held the door open for her, closing it when she got inside. Then rounded the vehicle, hopping in himself. But he didn't start the vehicle right away.

"I'd invite you to have a fish fry, but I don't want your brother to miss out on it either." And there would be no sex had with her brother in attendance.

"We don't even like fish."

Then why did they go fishing?

She must've seen the confusion on his face because she giggled, scooted to his side and placed a hand on his chest. "He snoozes, he loses. He should've never left if he wanted fish."

"So you both do like fish? You don't want me to invite him?"

Because otherwise Duke was confused as hell why they went fishing in the first place if neither liked it.

She kissed him instead of answering his question. It felt like she was trying to change the subject, and he didn't like that. But then her hand was rubbing his cock, and all train of thought left this mind. He didn't like fish at the moment either.

She had his jeans unbuttoned and the zipper down in a flash, snaking a hand around his cock, stroking it as if she knew every spot he loved. Because damn, she knew how to touch him.

He pulled her mouth away, breathing heavy. "Someone could pull in."

"They could." She stroked her hand down, then up, squeezing his cock with just the right amount of pressure. "Or we could quit talking about it, be quick and out of here before anyone else can arrive."

"Okay."

She didn't have to tell him twice, not when the pleasure was close to the top.

"You gotta stop, Noel, or I won't last."

"Or I can make you come twice." Then she lowered her mouth, sucking him hard.

"Shit!" He closed his eyes, growling in approval. He fumbled for the lever to the seat, moving it back. When he had enough room, he forced himself to pull her mouth away from his cock. "I need to be inside you, even though that was the most amazing feeling ever."

"Okay," she said, mimicking the one word and how he had said it moments before.

He dug his wallet out and the condom he packed, rolling it on while she shimmied out of her sweats and underwear. Then she was getting on his lap and sinking down onto him.

They both moaned in pleasure at the same time.

His lips found hers again, devouring her mouth as his hands gripped her hips, guiding her up and down. She increased the pace, riding him so fast and hard, the kiss they shared was messy to the point they stopped. She bent her head near his neck as he held her closer. As close as she could get, their bodies rubbing together in a beautiful way. The windows started to fog up as the heat rose in the vehicle.

"I'm so close," he whispered in her ear.

"Yes," was the answer he heard.

Then her lips attached to his neck, kissing and suckling as the grinding of their bodies intensified to newer heights. Until he growled in pleasure, tensing as the orgasm hit him. Teeth dug into his skin, which increased the bliss spreading across his body, her own beautiful moan left her lips as she came with him.

Damn.

He'd never been bitten before during sex, and he had to admit he liked it. A lot.

She lifted her head with a shyness spreading across her face. It looked so foreign on her as she had never been reserved with him before.

"I'm sorry. I got carried away. I didn't mean to bite you."

He cupped the back of her head, pressing a tender kiss to her lips. "I liked it. I need you to bite me again the next time."

"Next time?"

Had he overstepped? Been too presumptuous?

"If you want a next time."

He was still deep inside her. So when she grinded against him, he growled in approval at the contact.

"I want."

Okay, good. He hadn't been presumptuous.

"As much as it pains me, you should get off." He flickered a glance out the window. "We got lucky no one came."

"If you insist." She giggled as she got off his lap and grabbed her sweats and underwear.

"You're trouble, you know that?" He said it with a smile, so she'd know he was teasing. But she was trouble, getting him to have sex in such public places. Risking exposing themselves in such an intimate way. "This is the second time we've done this in public."

She lifted her hips as she pulled up her pants. "I bet we can find another great spot next."

He buttoned his jeans, leaned across the seat, and pulled her head closer. "Trouble with a capital T." Then he brushed his lips with hers, savoring the sweetness of her mouth. "Why don't we try a bed next? Like my place."

When she sighed, he backed away. Okay. He had crossed the invisible line between them. He'd stepped over casual and into serious? He wasn't positive, but he knew the sigh wasn't a good sign.

"I can't explain a good reason to my brother about coming over unless he knows why."

And it sounded like she didn't want him to know why. He wasn't sure he was too keen on the idea either.

"You invited us over for a fish fry. Is that still on the table?"

Anything was on the table if it meant he could see her again. That meant they did like fish, and he didn't have to worry about her lying to him for such an odd reason. "Yes. I would love to cook for you." He almost forgot. "And your brother."

She giggled. "Then it's a date. Whatever is good for you. Tonight we already made reservations for Rosetta's. We heard it has the best Italian in the area. So any night but tonight."

"It does. You will love it there." He started the truck. "I have off tomorrow. I can also do Thursday evening. Friday and the weekend is tough. I'll be working doubles because of Halloween and the festivities going on."

"Tomorrow night then. I'll even let you clean the fish."

That garnered a huge bout of laughter from him. "Because I guarantee you don't know how to clean them."

"Busted."

He grabbed another kiss because he couldn't help himself, and he needed to shore up as many kisses as he could since it would be a while before he got another.

"It's a date," he said as he brushed her lips, repeating the same words she used.

❄

She settled herself in the booth across from Nick and picked up the menu. Rosetta's had a nice atmosphere. Low lighting to give the romantic vibe, but not too low where a person felt they couldn't see anything properly. Light, airy music played in the background. All the staff wore black outfits, looking sharp and as if only rich people should eat here. Though a quick glance at the menu said the prices were decent.

It was two towns away from Sleighville and she felt like she had entered the real world again. Sleighville was...a lot. Everywhere you looked, Christmas was in your face. Here, in Bathington, reality was back.

"Good evening, my name is Stacy. Welcome to Rosetta's. Can I start you off with something to drink?"

"I'll stick with a water for now."

Her brother ordered an IPA. Then Stacy left, returning rather quickly with their drinks, along with a basket of bread and a side of an oily sauce. They needed a few more minutes to decide what to order, and the lady had ESP or something because she knew right at the exact moment they had decided they were ready to order.

Nick pointed at the menu. "I'm going to try the spaghetti. Fresh made noodles, uh?"

"You'll never want to go back to boxed noodles again," Stacy replied with a confident smile.

That good? They were told around Sleighville this place had the best Italian in the area. It was one reason they wanted to try it. She loved visiting new places and experiencing different dishes.

"I'm going to try the Bistecca alla Fiorentina." She felt like a hearty meal instead of pasta. And she could always snatch some of Nick's for a taste.

Stacy gave her a winning grin. "Excellent choice. You will love it."

Noel was impressed when Stacy walked away without even writing anything down. The woman was a genius, remembering everything. Not that they had given her a complicated order.

Five minutes later, Stacy came bearing another basket of bread, noticing they had devoured the entire basket and soaked up all the sauce. Some sort of olive oil mixture or something. Noel had no idea, but whatever it was had made her eat it all.

"You don't want to get too full before the main course, but you can always bring the bread home."

Noel chuckled, grabbing another piece. "You know I will. I won't even be shy to ask for another basket before we leave."

Stacy laughed along with her. "Where are you folks from? You don't sound from around here."

Noel knew they didn't even sound like they were from New York either. They'd moved around a lot as kids. New York had been the last stop, and they had never left.

"New York City," Noel replied. "But we're staying in Sleighville right now, enjoying the festivities." Noel held up a piece of bread. "I have to say that this bread beats Noel's Cafe, and I really like their food."

"Juliet makes the best food in that town. But yeah," Stacy said with a wicked twist of her lips as if they were sharing a secret. "I have to agree about the bread. We add a special ingredient, which is a secret, so I can't share what it is."

"If I actually made bread, I'd get it out of you," Nick said, jumping into the conversation.

"Maybe you would. Maybe you wouldn't." Stacy laughed, then turned serious in the blink of an eye. "Have

you heard about the poor woman who was murdered there?
She worked at Noel's Cafe."

"Bits and pieces. Not many folks have brought it up."
Noel was surprised Stacy did. But then again, some people
loved to gossip. No one, not one person in Sleighville, had
brought it up. Noel had to lie since they knew everything
about the murder.

"She was such a nice woman. Beth was her name."

Nick perked up in his seat, and Noel kicked him under
the table to not appear too interested in what she had to
stay.

"You knew her?" Noel asked casually.

"Oh, yeah. She came in here all the time. Sat at the bar.
She always looked so sad. We got to chatting, I can't help
myself." Stacy chuckled. "I hate when people look sad. I
always made a point to say hi and check in with her. At one
point, I even tried to convince her to quit the cafe and work
here. I told her I would've been able to get her hired here.
The manager loves me."

Stacy was turning out to be the best waitress in the
world.

"She didn't like working at the cafe? We had supper with
Juliet and her family the other night. She seemed so nice."

"Don't get me wrong. Juliet is nice. I know her myself.
Beth would never say what was bugging her. I didn't know if
it was her job at the cafe or something else."

"She always came here alone?" Nick prodded.

"Yep. Had a drink at the bar and a small meal. Lucian,
who runs the bar, had a sweet spot for her. Always gave her
a discount on the drinks and added more alcohol than he
should've." Stacy leaned in closer. "But I didn't tell you that."
Then she snapped her fingers. "One time when she was
here, an older gentleman came in. They seemed to know

each other. He was much older, like a grandfather figure. I don't know what they talked about, but she wasn't happy after he left. That was about a week before she..." Stacy trailed off, her eyes glazing over as if she got lost in her own thoughts. "She came in so regularly that when she didn't show up for two weeks, I popped into the cafe and asked about her. I was surprised to hear she up and left. It didn't feel like something she'd do. And I was right. She'd been killed. I feel like I failed her somehow."

Stacy shook her head as if throwing off the bad vibes that attacked her. "I am so sorry I brought up something so depressing. Forgive me."

She had done nothing wrong. In fact, she'd delivered their first actual good news. A direction to explore.

"It's fine. Truly."

Stacy nodded at Noel and turned around.

"Stacy?"

The woman twisted back toward her.

"You were a good friend to Beth. I'm sure she appreciated your kindness, your friendship. Remember that."

Stacy's eyes welled up with tears. "Thank you. I think I needed to hear that. Don't you worry, you're getting extra bread before you leave."

Then she winked before walking off.

Nick leaned closer, whispering, "I think we've been trying to dig into the wrong town."

"I think you're right. That's our first real lead."

Nick looked around as if casing the joint.

"What are you thinking?" Because her brother had been known to do stupid shit. He'd never been caught and arrested, but that gave him more confidence to do stupid stuff.

"They have cameras up."

"It was months ago. How do you know if they still have surveillance from that time?"

Nick smirked. "I won't know until I hack into their system."

Yep.

Her brother was going to doing something stupid.

8

SHE PLOPPED down on the couch next to her brother, jostling the cushions and garnering a frustrated growl out of him when it nearly made his computer fall off his lap.

"Do you mind?"

"Not at all," she replied cheekily as she peered at the screen.

A bunch of mumbo-jumbo computer code stared at her. She knew he was trying to break into the restaurant's security system.

They had an excellent meal last night at Rosetta's. They even stopped at the bar for one drink. To chat with Lucian.

He had been as open about Beth as Stacy had been. Unlike in Sleighville, they weren't afraid to question him and be subtle about it. He didn't seem to mind answering anything either.

Beth had been lonely and afraid of something, though he could never get her to admit about what. He even confessed to flirting with her and asking her out once. She had declined, telling him it wasn't the right time. In the future when she solved her dilemma, she'd love to.

But what had that meant? Dilemma?

Now, more than ever, she had wished Beth would've called her or picked up the phone when she called. She would've dropped everything to help her sister.

Lucian didn't recognize the man who dropped by, but he confirmed Stacy's version that he had upset her.

So if Lucian hadn't recognized him, did that mean he wasn't from around the area? From Sleighville? Were they looking for someone who had followed Beth to town and had already left? That would make their job even harder to find her killer.

But they left the restaurant feeling rejuvenated in their quest for justice. Nick grabbed his computer the moment they got back, trying to get into the security system. He failed.

This morning, they got up bright and early and headed back to Bathington and did their sightseeing there. In addition to questioning everyone they met. Of course, they didn't act like detectives on a case, but they made sure to bring up Beth at some point in the conversation. Everyone had been a wealth of information.

When Beth hadn't been working or hanging out in her rental place, she had been in Bathington. She did her shopping there, from groceries to clothes to anything else she needed. People said she was a nice, friendly woman who they couldn't believe got murdered. Unlike Stacy and Lucian, they didn't notice her sadness. They didn't notice her need to get away from something. Which told Noel she spent the most time at Rosetta's.

How had none of this information not been in the police's notes? Every other person they interviewed had been in her case file. Which meant, they left all this out...or they never thought to interview anyone from that town.

Nobody had ever seen anyone else with her in town. She always shopped alone. So their mystery man had only confronted her at the restaurant.

That was their next objective. Identify the man.

"How long do you think this will take?"

Nick glanced at her out of the corner of his eye, still maintaining the rapid speed of his fingers on the keyboard.

"A while, sis. I'm sorry it's not that easy hacking into shit."

"Excuse me," she drawled. "Do you remember me mentioning the fish fry at Duke's tonight? You know, the fish you didn't help catch."

"Oh, yeah, shit." He stopped typing and gave her his full attention. "This is important. We need to see this guy's face. You're not much help until I can get into the system. Go without me."

Her first response was to scream hell yeah and pump her fist into the air.

What she said instead was, "He expects you to be there."

Because she had made it known if her brother wasn't there he'd suspect they'd been getting it on. Duke would think it odd if he didn't show up and would assume Nick knew what was happening between them. But he didn't know, and she didn't intend for him to know.

"Do you want me to stop what I'm doing for fish? I hate salmon."

She rolled her eyes. "We're not having salmon. We didn't catch stupid salmon from the lake. We caught sunnies and one bass."

"Right. Whatever. If I hate salmon, I'm sure I hate that shit too."

"It'll be weird if you don't go. I can't tell him you're trying to hack into a security system. So I'm going to tell him you're stuck on the toilet with diarrhea."

Nick busted out laughing. "Why you gotta do that to me? Why?"

Noel stood up, shrugging nonchalantly but with a huge smirk. "Because I can. I'll eat extra fish for you."

And have some amazing sex once again. In a bed too, like Duke wanted.

"Whatever." Then he went back to the computer, tuning her out.

Noel left the room to get ready. Though she didn't change her clothes or doll herself up too much. She didn't want Nick to know she had a desire to impress Duke. She waved with her back to Nick and opened the door.

"Hey, Noel."

She glanced at her brother.

"Don't stay out too late. Be careful."

"Careful? Duke's not going to hurt me."

"I didn't think so when I left you with him to fish. But he's the one who signed off on all the documents in Beth's case file, which means he was the lead on her case. We found a big clue in her disappearance. It could lead us somewhere. Why didn't he find it?"

Duke wasn't the bad guy. She couldn't believe that. Refused to believe it.

"My gut says someone in this town—not Bathington—killed her. As much as I think the dude might be okay, we need to be careful about who we trust. Call me on your way home so I know when you're leaving."

"I will."

She wasn't even going to joke around about that. He worried about her. About her safety, even if she could protect herself. She would let him have his worry. But she was going to ignore what he said about Duke. She agreed someone in this town killed Beth. But that someone wasn't Duke.

They had exchanged numbers when Duke dropped her off at home yesterday. He'd texted her his address. Surprisingly, that was the sole communication between them.

Why was that surprising? It shouldn't be. They were having casual sex. A vacation fling—while she looked for her sister's killer. Nothing else would happen between them. He lived in a crazy Christmas town, and she was heading back to the big city when this was all done.

When she pulled into his driveway, she couldn't stop the silly laugh. It poured out as she walked on the pathway— lined with candy cane lights—to his front door. A merry wreath was hanging on the white door. The porch was strung up with multi-colored Christmas lights. And he had white icicle lights hanging from the gutters.

In October!

She rang the doorbell and it opened two seconds later as if he had been waiting by the door for her to arrive. With her brother, of course. He had no idea she would be coming alone.

A quick search told him one person was missing.

"Where's Nick?"

"Stomach issues. Barely could leave the bathroom for a minute and right back on the toilet."

Duke's expression said he felt bad for her brother. He shouldn't, especially since it was a bald-faced lie. She felt bad for lying to him, but it was a necessary evil. He couldn't know what her brother was up to.

She pointed a finger up, not letting him have a chance to express his dismay about Nick. "You're missing the ridiculous Santa and his reindeer on the roof. Your decorations aren't complete without that."

He waved her off, laughing. "I know. It's crazy to have the decorations up, but the tourists love it. People drive around town to see the Christmas lights. Do you know how many times I see cars slow down and take pictures of my house?"

"You'd get even more traffic if you added Santa up there."

Duke grabbed her arm, pulling her inside, and shut the door. Then he trapped her in place.

"Enough about Santa. I can't tell you how excited I am you came alone." His lips caressed hers. "Of course, I feel bad for your brother and his stomach."

She palmed his ass, pulling him closer. "Don't be. Don't even think about him."

Then his lips were on hers. This kiss wasn't soft and tender, but rough and hard. His tongue dove in and she matched his fiery pace.

She missed this, which was crazy because she'd seen him yesterday afternoon.

But his touch, the way he held her as if he never wanted to let go was a feeling she'd never felt. Duke was different from the other guys she'd slept with. In so many ways.

Her hand went for his jeans, unbuttoning them and yanking down the zipper. Then her hand snagged inside and wrapped around him.

He groaned against her mouth.

Then his hands were on her jeans, doing the same thing, but shoving hers down. In between the passionate twist of their lips and her stroking him in a frenzy, she managed to kick off her shoes, jeans, and underwear.

He pulled away, breathing heavily. "God, don't stop." He closed his eyes, savoring the way she touched him as his hand fumbled in his pocket. A handy condom appeared. Not in his wallet this time. What had this devilish man thought would happen with her brother in attendance?"

"Okay, you can stop," he murmured.

She let go and he covered his cock with the safety measure.

"Were you planning on stealing a moment away with me with my brother in the house?"

Duke grinned. "I wanted to be prepared for anything." He gripped her waist and lifted her up, then drove into her. "Especially when you surprise me at every turn. I have to be prepared for anything."

She bit her bottom lip, unable to contain a smile.

Then Duke was thrusting in and out, holding her solidly against the front of his door like he had at the bar. Again, she felt safe and secure his arms.

Every time he pumped into her, a glorious sensation rippled across her skin. She would never get tired of this. Get tired of the way Duke made her feel.

"Yes, Noel," he whispered, pressing his lips to her neck. "I feel you getting closer. Let go. Let me feel you squeeze me hard."

"You're such a dirty talker." She giggled, shivering at the way his soft kisses on her neck made her ticklish.

"That's not even anything." Then he moved his mouth to her ear, whispering even dirtier things that surprised her. He didn't seem like the type of guy to say such vulgar, dirty things. She loved it! Then he nipped the bottom of her lobe and it sent a shot of ecstasy through her body.

He pounded harder into her as the intense orgasm swept her away. She even screamed his name. Because for the first time, she didn't have to be quiet. Not that she had to be quiet at the lake, but she had felt like she had to be more reserved there. Here, she knew she could be as loud and as wicked as she wanted to be.

Duke thrusted a few more times before letting go himself.

Their heavy breathing filled the space.

"So much for utilizing a bed."

Duke chuckled, snatching a kiss before letting her down gently. "Well, it's early and we have all night to find my bed."

Oh. She loved that he was insinuating they would be having more fun in other rooms in the house.

"But first, let's eat some fish."

The sinful grin on his face had her willing to do anything that he wished to do.

DUKE FORKED the last piece of fish on his plate, shoving it into his mouth. He'd done a damn good job frying the fish. The side dish had been simple though. Potato chips. Fish and chips. Noel had gotten a giggle out of that when he told her.

Of course, before he could start frying up the fish, the way she laughed, the way her happiness filled him up, he'd reached for her. That started another round of lovemaking.

Against his kitchen counter.

That was a first for him. Like the supply closet at the bar. The front of his door. He couldn't claim having sex in a vehicle was new to him. He'd lost his virginity in the back-seat of a car.

Once they'd sated themselves again, they redressed for the second time, and he started cooking. He had to say he loved the view next to him at the table.

She wasn't a dainty eater. He dated a woman like that

one time and it had driven him nuts watching her eat. But Noel wasn't shy about food, shoveling in bites, moaning at times, telling him how much she loved it.

"Nick missed out. I'm going to rub it in."

Duke laughed, putting his fork down. All his fish was gone. "Don't do that to him. That'd be cruel when he had no choice in the matter."

The smile on her face maintained its composure, but he could see some of it dim in her amber-colored eyes. As if she was holding something back. That his comment had bothered her. What had he said wrong?

"You didn't tell me how good Rosetta's food would be." She leaned in as if they weren't alone and she had to be quiet. "Don't tell Juliet that her bread does not beat theirs."

More laughter left his mouth. "I think she knows that. She's tried to con them out of the recipe for the last two years. I'm glad you guys enjoyed it. What'd you do today?"

Again, her eyes flashed uncertainty before her smile inched up a notch. Odd.

"We roamed around Bathington. After eating at Rosetta's, we wanted to see more of it. Cute town. Nice change of pace from all the Christmassy stuff."

"You get used it."

She pursed her lips in a comical way. "I doubt that." Her sweet laughter filled the air. "And how was your day?"

"Not bad. I had lunch at the cafe. Before I left the area, a kid tried to shoplift from Shannon's store. She ended up giving him the shirt for free and didn't want to press charges. I don't think he's going to learn anything."

Noel picked up her glass of white wine, taking a sip. "Everyone deserves a second chance."

"And how do I know if this was his second chance? It could've been his fourth or fifth for all I know."

"Maybe, but with you, it was his first time. With her, it was his first time. He now has a second chance with both of you. Maybe he needed that one person to do so. You don't know his past. You don't know what he's been through or why he might've wanted—or needed—to steal that shirt."

Her answer felt like it had a deeper meaning. That he should be paying attention to every word.

"Do you have cards?"

At the random question, his mind shook off the unease that wanted to take over. "Yeah, why?"

"Let's play some poker." She bit her bottom lip with a sly smile hiding behind the adorable gesture. "Make the betting some fun."

By that, she meant strip poker.

Damn, she was far better at cards than he expected. He lost more clothes before her. Of course, the cards scattered around the living room after a few hands because they had more important things to do. Like devour each other.

They had another round of sex in his living room.

Amazing, life-altering sex.

He couldn't remember a time he'd had sex so many times in one night. He couldn't believe how much he couldn't get enough of her and vice versa.

They sat on the floor, leaning against the couch, naked, drinking their wine.

"Why haven't we made it to a bed yet?" she asked with a goofy grin.

"That is a wonderful question. I have no idea. The night is still young."

She finished her glass and set it on the coffee table near her. He'd moved it before their intense lovemaking had started. One minute they were on the couch, and then they were tumbling to the floor. Noel had nearly hit her head on the end of the table.

"I need to use the bathroom." She stood up, grabbing her clothes, telling him she planned on getting dressed.

Seemed ridiculous if they were going to have round four in his room, but he didn't say anything. He didn't want to be presumptuous that round four would happen. Though he had a feeling it would.

"I'll refill your glass."

She glanced at it, pressing her lips together hard. "Not a whole lot. I do have to drive back home."

Shit. He wished she didn't have to. But that would tell her brother what they'd been doing, and he knew she didn't want that getting out. Neither did he. Not to her brother, anyway.

"You got it."

Duke dressed himself before snagging both their glasses and heading to the kitchen where he'd left the bottle. He filled his to the same level as hers. About a quarter full. Because she was right. Not too much if she had to drive. He wanted to be at the same level of lucidity as her.

He ventured back to the living room, putting the coffee table back into place. No need for it to be on the side of the couch because the next spot for sex would be his bed. He'd make sure of it. A nice, soft comfortable bed where he could take his time exploring. Kissing every part of her body before they even got to the good stuff.

A glance at his watch said it'd been over five minutes since she left the room. What was taking her so long? Had he hurt her somehow? Too much sex?

He stood up and made his way down the hallway. He didn't even make it to the bathroom because he saw her in his spare room.

Damn.

Looking at something she shouldn't be looking at.

"Noel…"

She didn't turn away from the wall that was plastered with everything he had on Beth's case. Even the photos of her body after they'd pulled it from the lake.

He stopped next to her. "You shouldn't be in here."

"You tensed when I mentioned going to Tinsel Lake. This is why."

Yes, damn it!

"Why didn't you tell me a body was pulled out of it?"

"Because I didn't want to frighten you. I don't think…I don't think she was killed there."

Noel turned her head toward him. "So someone was murdered in this town and you didn't tell me that either. You think the person dumped her body there?"

"I think so." He had no excuse why he didn't mention the murder to her. It wasn't a conversation he wanted to have to begin with. Murder was not a light topic, especially for what he wanted to do with her. More sex in his bedroom.

"Why do you have all this up here? In your house?" She waved her hand wildly in the air, gesturing at the wall.

Not even Griffin knew he'd set up shop in his spare room, intending to work her case until he solved it.

"Because I'm not stopping until I find who killed her. She deserves that."

Noel stared at him as if confused by it all.

With a touch of heartache.

Okay, they were having the tough conversation.

"Her name is Beth Terden. She worked at Noel's cafe for three months before she up and left. At least, that's what we all assumed. Her rental place was cleared of her belongings and that was enough cause to say she'd skipped town. We found her body in May, telling us we'd been wrong. It's my first murder case I've ever had. Which isn't surprising because Sleighville does not generally have murders. I've tried my best, but it's hard to work a case when there's no evidence to help you along. The water deteriorated any possible evidence that could've been on her body. The place she lived at was already occupied by someone new. Worthless to search for prints, though I did do another sweep of the place in case I missed something, and I didn't find anything. I tried my best. And I'm going to keep trying my best. I refuse to admit defeat. Because after the way we all assumed the worst of her, she deserves justice."

"If you're trying your best, that's all you can do. Don't blame yourself for the lack of evidence."

Yeah, well, that was easier said than done.

"Come on. You shouldn't be in here. It is an official investigation."

"And I shouldn't see any of this. I get it. It's getting late. I should go."

"Right."

Not to mention looking at a dead, bloated body was a mood killer.

He walked her to the door and got a brief kiss. She pulled away faster than he liked. But he knew why. What she had seen disturbed her. He understood that well. It disturbed him every morning when he walked into the room.

He didn't say he'd call her and she didn't offer the same sentiment. She walked to her car and didn't look toward his front door once before pulling out of his driveway and leaving.

What a shitty way to end what had been a wonderful evening.

He downed his glass of wine, then hers. That wasn't enough.

Instead of refilling his glass, he grabbed a beer. He only had wine in the house because that's what she'd drank at Griffin's house. He wanted her to have what she liked, not what he liked.

Settling into his bed, he rested his head against the wall.

Next time he had a woman over, he needed to remember to close his spare room door.

Definite mood killer.

9

SHE SHUT the cottage door with a quiet click, still in a daze.

The moment she passed the room, she had to backtrack to see if her eyes had been playing tricks on her. She'd gone past it the first time without glancing at it, using the bathroom and getting dressed. On the way back, her eyes had wandered a fraction of a second. Enough time to make her pause.

Walking into that room had thrown her off. It had been one thing to see all the case file information on a computer screen. It was another thing to see it all up on display on a wall. Especially pictures of her body. She had always skipped that part in the file. She assumed Nick had as well, though she had never asked.

"Noel?"

She looked up at her brother as her eyes had been trained on the floor. She hadn't made it very far into the room either. The door had closed and she'd stopped, her purse dangling in her hand.

"What's the matter?"

She walked in a trance, still stuck in the same mode as

when she left Duke's. She didn't even know how she left his house as normal as she did without tipping him off. Or how she made it home in one piece. She didn't remember a moment of the drive.

Her butt plopped down next to her brother. He moved his computer off his lap and to the coffee table, turning toward her.

"Did he hurt you?"

"No."

How did she begin to tell Nick what she saw?

He grabbed her hand and cupped her chin. "What the hell is wrong? You look like you've seen a ghost or something."

"Have you ever looked at Beth's body? The crime scene photos."

His hand dropped from her face, but he still kept ahold of her hand. "One time. It's not pretty."

"I know." Her eyes blurred as the images came back to her as if she were looking at them again. "Duke has a whole room filled with the stuff from her case. I saw it by accident, after using the bathroom. It's horrible. She looked..."

A cry tore out of her.

Nick squeezed her hand. "Don't think about it."

"It's impossible not to." A tear slid down her cheek. "I don't like lying to him. I can't lie to Duke anymore."

"We have no choice."

"No, we do. We should tell him what information we found yesterday. The security camera footage. He could get a copy without any issue."

Nick laughed mercifully. "And then after we do, he'll arrest my ass for trying to hack into the system. You're not thinking clearly right now. We can't tell him anything."

"I can't lie to him. It's not right. I can't—" The tears burst out of her.

Nick shoved her into his arms, holding tight. "It's okay, Noel. I promise you, it will all be okay. I swear."

It didn't feel okay. Nothing felt normal or sane anymore.

Nick knew that, so she didn't respond, despite his many repeating of the same thing. That it would all be okay.

She cried in his arms until nothing was left inside of her. Nick knew she had no energy for anything. Because this wasn't the first time she'd broken down before. Nor the first time he had to take care of her because she couldn't do it herself. He picked her up and carried her to the bedroom, pulling off her shoes and tossing them to the floor.

He left the room and returned with a glass of water and two pills. Her brother knew her so well. That she had a massive headache after the heavy crying she'd unleashed. She always got a headache from it.

She took the pills on autopilot, then let him tuck her in like she was five years old. He'd always been there for her. He'd always be there for her.

Her eyes closed and she fell asleep.

The next morning when she woke up, the headache was still there. Not surprising. Nor was the fact two more pills were on the nightstand with another glass of water. Her brother knew it wouldn't be gone yet.

She took them and laid there another few minutes before dragging herself out of bed. Her first stop was the bathroom. To use the toilet, then the shower. She felt marginally better after the hot water soothed her bones.

After dressing in a pair of sweats and a T-shirt, she ventured into the other room. Breakfast was waiting on the table for her. Nick sat across from the empty seat.

He didn't say a word until she had polished off most of the eggs, bacon, and toast she'd eaten.

"How you feeling?"

Not up to full strength yet. When she got into these moods, it was hard to get herself out of them.

"Okay. Thanks for taking care of me."

He reached across the table and grabbed her hand. "I will always take care of you, Noel. Until I die. You know that." His brows were in a tight line as were his lips. "I think you should go back home."

"And you're going to stay?"

He let go of her hand and snatched his computer that was to the side, turning the screen toward her. He'd managed to hack into the system. Not surprising. Her brother was a genius with a computer. An older gentleman, like a grandfather type that Stacy had said, stood next to Beth at the bar, his face twisted in anger.

"We can't tell Duke anything. Because now I've managed to get into the system, and I don't want to go to jail. I will keep looking for this guy to question him. But I think you should go home."

"I'm not leaving you."

Nick sighed. "If we run into Duke again, you're going to have a hard time lying to him. Even more so now. He might be a good guy—"

"He is!" How could her brother not see that? "He feels responsible for Beth. He feels guilty he can't solve it, and he shouldn't. He doesn't have much to go on."

"Well, he didn't interview anyone in Bathington."

"And why would he think he had to go two towns over from Sleighville to do so? We know Beth was hiding something, which meant she was hiding it from everyone in this town. He had no reason to believe she was going there so often. Not if anyone didn't know." She slouched into her chair, sighing. "He'd have a new lead if we told him about what we found."

"Not yet. I want to do my own digging. That's why we came here."

"Nick..."

He stood up. "You relax and rest. I'm going to town for a few supplies and I'll be back."

She didn't have the energy to argue with him.

His few supplies had been more than she expected. Five bags of candy and two Halloween costumes. His grin widened when she looked at him as if he'd lost his mind.

"Tomorrow is Halloween, Noel. We are not missing the fun around here. Eve and Griffin mentioned the other night they get tons of trick-or-treaters on this street. We'll stay in today. Regroup and rejuvenate ourselves. Then tomorrow we have some fun with trick-or-treaters, and after that, we'll get back right into the hunt."

She hoped like hell she'd have her mojo back. The will to keep fighting. It was hard to find the strength when all she saw in her mind was Beth's dead body. She should've never stepped inside that room.

Nick pulled the costumes out of the bags, and she couldn't stop laughing. For a good solid minute.

"Mr. and Mrs. Claus? Really? That's the best you could do."

"Hey," he said with a chuckle. "The store didn't have much left to rent, okay? I did my best." He patted the front of Mrs. Claus's outfit. "It even comes with extra padding."

"Yes, because they're both plump individuals." She rolled her eyes, but then she smiled because she knew her brother was trying to lighten the mood. Make her feel better. Make her forget the horrors she saw.

"Let's watch some scary movies today. Get us in the Halloween spirit."

Well, then she needed her comfort scary movies. The ones she could watch over and over and knew every single second of it. "Can we start with *Halloween H2O*?" It was her favorite out of the franchise.

Nick rolled his eyes this time. "Yeah, of course we can. So you can drool over the main male character like you always do."

It would help distract her.

That's what she needed right now.

DUKE HAD his friendly officer smile on his face, yet his internal mood was swirling with chaos.

He hadn't seen or spoken to Noel since Wednesday night. Yesterday, being Halloween, he thought he'd at least see her around town. There had been quite a few festivities going on before the sun set and the trick-or-treaters came out.

Except he hadn't seen her once. Not even Nick.

He knew they hadn't left town because he couldn't help himself but drive by the cottage to confirm it. When he got home from working a double, he'd crashed. Only to get up less than eight hours later to do it again.

Now the parade was moving along, and he kept scanning the crowds to see a glimpse of her. Or her brother.

And nothing. Not one sighting.

Though, to be fair, the streets were filled up and down with people. Lila had done it again. Their first official Halloween parade was a massive success. Marching bands, local businesses, and anyone else who paid to have a float in the parade filled the streets. More candy was given out to the hungry kids as if they hadn't gotten enough last night.

Poor parents dealing with all that sugar high.

Duke wanted to see Noel and see what she thought of Santa dressed up as a clown. A little spooky, in his opinion, especially for the younger kids, but nobody seemed to be bothered by it. Lots of pointing and laughing at his costume. Santa's makeup wasn't spooky, but Duke had never been a fan of clowns, so to him, it gave off a creepy vibe.

The parade was half over. After this, there would be tents and booths, and a beer garden set up in the church's parking lot for more fun and entertainment. He'd be having another long day into the night.

He'd have to see Noel at some point.

Of course, he had her number. He could text her. Yet, she hadn't texted him either. They weren't exclusive or a couple. It was a fling.

Casual sex.

Considering he had never engaged in such an affair before, he didn't know all the rules of engagement. Did he text? Did he wait to run into her again? How did he respond, especially after the way she left his house? Not mad at him, but things had been odd and strained.

All because she'd walked into a room she should've never set eyes on to begin with.

"How's it going?"

Duke maintained his smile at Bryce's greeting.

"Crowd is mellow, but cheerful, so it's going great. Lila is a genius."

Bryce beamed with pride. "She is."

"How are your rounds going?" Because Duke knew, as mayor, Bryce loved to meet new people and chat with the townsfolk as much as he could.

"Excellent. As you said, mellow but cheerful crowd." Bryce's exuberant expression filled the space, removing some of the gloom Duke had carried around with him. "I hear you had supper with the people in the cottage next to Grif. I have yet to meet them and I want to."

Like that, his mood plummeted once again, not that he gave Bryce any indication he didn't want to talk about them.

"Yeah, it was a nice time."

"And you went fishing with Noel."

"Good thing too because as city folks, they had no clue what they were doing."

Bryce laughed with him.

"And you cooked the fish...for just her."

Damn.

Rumors were swirling.

"I invited them both. Her brother had a stomach bug or something."

Bryce bobbed his head, but his wily smirk said he didn't believe any of that. Then he clapped Duke on the shoulder. "It's okay to have some fun, Duke. You, of all people, need more fun in your life. You work too much."

So he'd been hearing lately.

Then Bryce moved on, greeting more people in the crowd, while Duke went into search mode again.

Still no sign of Noel.

The parade ended with the crowd cheering loudly at it all. Then they dispersed, moving to the church lot.

Where the drinking started and the laughter and loud cheers continued. Well into the night.

His feet hurt. His back ached. And his heart was sore from all the worrying that plagued him.

Still no sign of Noel or Nick. All day long. At any part of the parade or church parking lot.

Lila found him brooding near the exit as people vacated the premises. It all ended in ten minutes. So the more people left on their own, the better for him and the rest of the crew on duty.

"You should be very proud of yourself."

Lila beamed with pride. "I am, Duke. It sounds conceited, but I am."

"Nope. Not at all. You've done wonders here, and I don't think anyone else could've pulled off what you did in a few short months. I haven't seen crowds like this in the longest time."

"Do you work tomorrow? I've seen you everywhere the last few days, from morning until night."

Duke laughed. "Ditto! You need to take tomorrow off. I have a short shift in the morning, but that's it. Then I have the next three days off."

In that timeframe, he would check on Noel. He didn't like that he hadn't seen her once in the past two days when he was used to seeing her around town for the past week.

Then someone was hollering Lila's name and she was off.

It took another hour to clear the place, and by the time Duke got home from clocking out, he was dead tired.

Of course, he had to be up again in less than eight hours for another shift. He felt like a zombie all morning until he made it back home where he crashed into bed. It wasn't until after five o'clock when he rolled out of bed. He'd slept far longer than he had intended.

First, he needed a shower, then he'd go check on Noel.

He hoped like hell he wasn't crossing an invisible line with her. With the causal thing they had going on.

10

"Umm...I'll take two turkey club sandwiches and two bowls of the chicken wild rice soup."

Noel didn't recognize the lady behind the counter. Not that she'd been in the cafe a whole ton, but it had always been the same people working every time, so it was a bit jarring to see someone new behind the counter.

She and Nick had enjoyed the parade yesterday. From the few parts they saw anyway. Their main objective had been searching the crowd for their mystery man. With no luck. They even went to the festivities at the church, keeping an eye out for him. When they struck out there, they decided to go to Bathington and show his picture to some of the same people they had already questioned. Nick had gone to the library to print off a still photo of the best angle from the video of the man.

No one recognized him. No one but the people at Rosetta's, where they had gone again. Spoke to Stacy, the waitress, and Lucian, the bartender, seeing if they could remember anything else about the interaction, about Beth. They couldn't provide anything else useful. Like a name for the guy.

Which, of course, hit her hard.

They were hitting wall after wall after wall, and it wasn't doing anything to help the mood she'd fallen in. Off and on she would lose her train of thought, letting her mind wander to the photos on Duke's wall. Every time, her brother had to pull her out of it.

She wished like hell she could wipe the images from her mind.

This morning when she woke up, she lounged in bed far longer than she should've. Nick knew when to get in her face and when to leave her alone. He gave her most of the morning to rise on her own. Right before she would've plunged deep into the recessives of her mind, he walked into the room and made her get up. Saved her from herself.

They were nearing the end of their stay. She could feel it. Because with no new leads, what were they to do.

While she wanted to question the people in Sleighville point blank, she knew Duke would be on her in an instant. She couldn't have that happen. He'd hate her forever for her lies.

The only thing she could be thankful for in the past few days was she hadn't run into him. She hadn't had the need to lie to his face. Because she didn't think she could. Not anymore.

Nick had skills, but there was even some stuff he wasn't capable of doing, at least not in the timeframe they wanted it done. So this afternoon, he'd sent the photo of the gentleman to another hacker friend who could run a facial recognition program on the photo. Get them a name. Hopefully in a decent time frame where they wouldn't have to stick around waiting forever. They'd interview the guy and get some answers.

While Nick had been busy doing his own sleuthing on the computer, she offered to get supper for them. Neither felt like cooking.

So here she was waiting for a meal she knew would be delicious.

The woman, Marcy, her name tag read, handed her the bag of food and wished her a great evening.

Not sure how great it would be, though she smiled and returned the sentiment. No need to throw all her problems on a complete stranger.

The town was still pretty busy from all the people who'd come for the parade and festivities yesterday, so she hadn't managed to find a spot to park on the street. She had to park in the lot by the church, walking a few blocks and cutting through the alleyway to get to Noel's Cafe.

With the sun setting, with the cool air, it gave her the chills as she headed back to her car. The only nice thing was the streets were filled with people.

People who had no worries on their mind. Not like the ones she had. Of course, everyone worried about something. But not like her. Wondering who killed her sister. Who could do something so cruel as to strangle her then dump her body in a lake like she was a piece of trash.

Images of Beth's body flooded her mind again.

Vacant eyes.

Marks around her neck.

She turned the corner and entered the alley.

The rope hanging off her feet.

She grunted in pain, dropping the bag in her hand when someone slammed her into the bricks, shoving her face into the rough wall. Her arm was twisted behind her back, making her cry out in pain. The person grabbed her around the neck, pushing her even harder into the wall, and squeezed with all his strength.

It restricted her air flow. She couldn't breathe. He'd been on her so fast, she had no time to react and fight back.

Hot breath hit her ear.

"Stop digging into Beth Terden's case."

His fingers tightened on her neck. She started coughing, trying to breathe.

"If you don't, you'll be next."

Then he let go of her neck and slammed her head into the bricks. She crumbled to the ground, losing consciousness.

When she reopened her eyes, night had descended. She had no idea how long she'd been out. Her head rang with pain, her throat hurt, and her arm hadn't been broken, but the twisting of it made it ache.

She walked to her car on autopilot, reminiscent of the way she'd been four days ago. Somehow, she started the car and started driving.

When she stopped the vehicle, she wasn't surprised where she'd ended up, though she should've been. Her mind had wandered again. But her instincts had taken her to the place she needed to be.

To the person she needed.

Duke.

Her legs held her up as she walked to his door, but she could feel her energy waning.

She hit the doorbell.

It opened a short time later.

"Holy shit, Noel!"

She stumbled into his arms, closing her eyes as he

wrapped her into his warm embrace. She was safe and secure. She always felt safe and secure in his arms.

"What the hell happened? Who did this to you? Did Nick—"

"No." She gripped the back of his shirt so hard she knew her nails scrapped his back. "Nick would never."

He pulled her away from him, examining her. "You need to go to the hospital."

"No!" This time she gripped the front of his shirt, the desperation surging in her veins. "No, please, no, Duke."

Then she burst into tears.

He swooped her into his arms, shut the door with his foot, and carried her to the couch. Her tears turned into sobs as he held her. Not one word left his mouth while he held her. Not even whispering words of comfort.

She appreciated that because nothing would comfort her. She had to get the tears out before she could find her voice and tell him what happened. Even then, she knew it would be difficult.

When they slowed to a stop, they sat there a few more minutes in silence.

Duke's fingers glided across her neck, no doubt eyeing the bruise left behind. Then he tipped her chin up.

"I need you to tell me what happened."

"I…" She couldn't find her voice. Not yet.

How stupid could she be? Letting someone sneak up on her. She had no chance to fight back. After all the training she'd put herself through and she'd been defenseless. As defenseless as her sister.

"You'll hate me. You're going to hate me." She dropped her head onto his chest, unable to look him in the eyes any longer.

He didn't respond. Probably confused as hell by what she was saying, *and* what she wasn't saying.

Then he stood up and carried her to the bathroom. He cleaned the wound on her forehead, no doubt given to her when the assailant slammed her so hard into the brick wall she'd lost consciousness. She also had a scrape on her cheek when he'd shoved her face into the wall. There was nothing he could do about the bruise on her neck, though his fingers brushed it, his body trembling as he did.

"I need you to tell me what happened."

Duke hadn't said much to her but repeat the same statement. She didn't know how to tell him. Where did she begin? Because she couldn't tell him what happened without telling him everything.

"Take me home, please. To Nick."

Why had she come here? This had been a bad idea. But she knew her limitations. There was no way she'd be able to drive home. She had no idea how she made it to Duke's in one piece.

He pressed his lips together as if he had to hold back what he wanted to say, then sighed.

"Fine. Maybe he'll tell me what the hell happened."

NOEL WAS quiet in the seat next to him, staring out the window. She'd gone quiet after his last terse sentence to her that her brother would tell him what happened. He knew he'd spoken too harshly.

But the moment he saw her battered and bruised, he'd lost it. His gut twisted in pain, envisioning who could've hurt her and what he'd do to the person when he got ahold of them. To see her like that...it had scared the hell out of him.

All he wanted was answers, and she wouldn't give them to him.

He pulled into the driveway and shut the car off. He'd driven her rental, and he'd find a ride home once he got the answers he sought. When he got out of the car and noticed she didn't exit, he had to help her out. She was looking at him but not really seeing him. Her eyes were glazed over as if she'd fled to a place in her mind.

He knocked on the door, holding Noel with his arm around her waist. Partly because he needed to be touching her in any way, and partly because he was afraid she wouldn't be able to hold herself upright.

Nick opened the door, zooming in on his sister right away.

"Noel!"

Nick pulled her roughly out of his arms and he didn't have it in him to argue. What would be the point? Nick guided his sister to the couch, making her sit down. Duke stepped inside and shut the door, walking closer to them, but didn't sit down. There wasn't room anyway since it was a loveseat.

Nick glared at him. "What the hell happened?"

He shrugged. "I don't know. I opened my door to the same thing. She won't tell me what happened. All she said was that I would hate her. I don't even know what that means."

By the way Nick averted his gaze right away, he knew what Noel meant. They were hiding something. He'd had moments where his gut gurgled with unease, but now it was flaring like a large siren going off. How had he missed this?

Well, hell.

He knew how.

He'd been blinded by lust.

"She left an hour ago to get us some food." Nick looked at his computer screen, though it was turned away from Duke so he didn't know what he was looking at. "Actually, it's been almost two hours. I lost track of time. I didn't realize she was gone so long."

Nick's hands trembled as he touched Noel's neck with a feathery caress. "Sis, you gotta tell me what happened."

Her lips trembled as if she were on the verge of crying again. God, Duke hoped not. He didn't like witnessing her tears the first time.

"Noel, you have to."

"Duke will—"

"He's not going to hate you or whatever you're thinking." Nick smoothed a path down her arms. "You were right. I was wrong. Okay. We should've told him everything a few days ago. Because that's what this is about, isn't it?" Nick's eyes filled with tears. "He tried to kill you too."

She jerked her head up and down once and winced. Duke knew the bruises on her neck caused it.

What had these two been up to? What did he mean by someone tried to kill her...too?

"He told me to stop looking into it. That if I didn't, I'd be next." She gripped his arms. "I can't—"

Nick nodded, as if he understood what his sister was saying. Duke was still confused as hell. About it all.

"Go lie down. I'll handle it."

Noel left the room, not looking at him once.

Nick stood up and gestured for him to follow. "I need a beer for this. Want one?"

"I want to take your sister to the hospital."

Duke sat at the table, ignoring the beer Nick set in front of him. Nick downed half the bottle he'd grabbed before letting it hit the table with a loud thud.

"I'm going to start at the beginning, and I need you to hear me out before you interrupt. Okay?"

Duke didn't think he had much of a choice. He'd treat this like an interrogation. His suspect was about to open up. No way in hell he'd interrupt before the full confession was complete. "Fine."

"We moved around a lot as kids, settling in New York City. Our mom did the best she could with the situation she was in. But she was weak. She wasn't strong enough. She got hit by a car and died."

Holy shit. Noel had said her mom died when she was a kid, and he had never bothered to ask how. That was tragic.

"To this day, I don't know if it was an accident or if she intentionally walked in front of it. It doesn't matter, I guess. That left us alone with our dad. Real asshole. He beat me more than Noel, but because I made sure he did. I tried to protect her as much as I could. She doesn't want to go to the hospital because we've been there too many times. And yeah, you're probably wondering why we never tattled on him to child protective services or the police. I thought about it a time or two, but they would've split us up in foster care and I wasn't going to let that happen. I picked the lesser of two evils. The bastard died of a heart attack when I turned eighteen. Noel was fifteen. I became her legal guardian. I would do anything for my sister. I know her inside and out. I know what she needs and when she needs it. Right now, she does not need you hating her for anything I'm about to tell you. Because if you so much as make her cry, you will be the sorriest man alive."

Duke believed every word Nick said. That he'd protect his sister in any possible way. He'd threatened an officer of the law.

But what Nick didn't know was that Duke would never hate Noel. That he'd also do anything for her as well.

"I won't hate her."

Maybe he should've voiced that to her back at his house when she whispered it. A huge error on his part.

"When Noel turned sixteen we got a surprise. Our sister —half-sister—knocked on our door, introducing herself. Not surprising that our deadbeat dad would cheat on our mom, but that we had a sister. Her own mom had died and she was all alone. The birth certificate she gave us proved we shared the same dad. Not sure how she found us because she would never tell me, but she did and she needed a place to stay. She was fifteen. A year younger than Noel, and now I had two sisters I had to take care of. Because that's what I do. I take care of my family. I would have never turned her away."

Duke had no idea where this story was going. He wanted Nick to get to the point so he could check on Noel.

"Our half-sister is Beth Terden."

"Excuse me?" Duke straightened in his seat. He had to have misheard.

"You heard me correctly. Let me finish," Nick said, gritting his teeth, a slight tick in his cheek. "Noel was close with Beth. Much closer than me. Not for the lack of trying. Beth was always closed-off, keeping things to herself. She up and left one day. Didn't tell either one of us. It hit Noel hard. Like, I'm talking really hard where she went out of her mind crazy with worry. Beth wouldn't pick up the phone, wouldn't return her calls. Nothing. We had no idea why she left like she did. She called me once after a week she'd been gone. Said she had to get away for a while and she'd be back when she was back. Noel was pissed she called me and not her. But I knew why Beth called me. Because I wouldn't get on her case about it, and Noel would. She'd want to help with whatever she needed help with.

"Months go by and Noel's constantly calling her and not getting an answer. Hell, I was starting to get worried myself. But I didn't do anything. I was giving Beth the space she wanted. Then it turned into over a year, and I could see the toll it was taking on Noel. The wondering, the worrying...so I ran a program—" Nick paused, as if reading his confused expression. "I'm a tad good with computers and code and shit. Anyways, I ran a program that would pop up Beth's name if it appeared on social media or anything. Imagine my shock when I saw her body had been found in a lake."

Nick blew out a harsh breath and took a long swallow of his beer.

"That was two weeks before we came here that I found that. It took me one week to show Noel. I didn't have the nerve right away because I knew it would devastate her. It took another week to try and comfort my sister and failing miserably at it. She then tells me she's coming to this town to find Beth's killer. To find her justice. Of course, I'm not letting my sister come here alone. So I went along with the idea. And here we are."

Was that Duke's cue that he could speak now? That he could interrupt? Give his rebuttal? He didn't know where to start. At the beginning seemed best, like Nick had.

"I tried locating next of kin. I couldn't find any. The address on her driver's license, when I contacted them, they said she hadn't lived there for two years." He still had no reason for why she never updated her address on her license, but now he knew why he couldn't locate next of kin. He had no idea she had half-siblings. Different last names so it would've been impossible to know she had family out there. Both her parents were dead.

"Beth moved around a lot. She even crashed at my place or Noel's more often than having her own place. She had a hard time settling anywhere."

"Why didn't you come to the police department the moment you got into town?"

"Well, Officer Fisk, because someone in this town killed my sister and I don't know who."

Duke laughed. "Not a cop."

"Oh, because all cops are good? Really? Are you sure about that?"

He wasn't wrong, but Duke knew no one in the police department was a killer. Not the people he worked side-by-side with. They couldn't be.

Though, to be fair, Bryce didn't think his secretary could turn out to be a killer and that had shocked the whole town. He could see Nick's point of view—as much as it pained him.

And hell.

Noel had been lying to him from the beginning. Now he understood why she thought he'd hate her. Not just from the lying.

She'd had sex with him.

She'd been playing him from the beginning.

"We found something a few days ago."

Duke perked up, forgetting why he shouldn't hate her. She deserved to be hated.

"When we went to Rosetta's. Did you know Beth went to that town a lot? Like, a lot."

He was unaware of that. Did that make him a horrible police officer? Yep. Being outsmarted by people not even law enforcement.

"The staff told us she argued with someone the week before she disappeared. I don't want to get arrested, but I am going to share with you what we found. I assume us asking more questions is what got Noel attacked tonight. Because we're getting close to the truth and that person doesn't want us doing that. I'll do anything to protect my sister, even if it means you gotta do your job and arrest me."

"Show me what you got."

Duke hadn't decided if he'd arrest him or not. He was feeling pretty pissed at the moment.

Nick got up, went to the living room, grabbed something and walked back to the table, setting his computer down. A photo glared at him. One of Beth and an older gentleman.

"This happened a week before she went missing. Everyone we spoke to said it was a pretty heated argument. You can tell from the video he's pretty upset. We've been trying to find him and question him. We have no idea who he is."

"This is a video?" It looked like a photo.

Nick tapped a few keys and then Duke saw what it was. Surveillance from a security camera.

"How did you get this? Rosetta's gave this to you?"

Nick grinned, then winced. "Not exactly."

Right. The part where he'd arrest him.

"When did you get this information?"

"A few days ago."

"And Noel wanted to bring it to me?" Duke remembered what Nick had said to her before he told her to leave the room.

"Yes."

Well, at least she had that going for her.

Duke stood up. "You should've listened to her." He pointed at the screen. "Because I know who that is."

11

DUKE BLEW OUT A BREATH, trying to find his composure before knocking on Griffin's door. He'd been hit with a huge blow tonight.

Finding out how terrible of an officer he was.

Realizing he'd been used by a woman.

Hating how much it hurt him to walk away from her despite the anger swirling in his veins because of her lies.

But he needed to address this. Now.

He demanded Nick email him a copy of the video and everything they'd found out so far. Duke had been shocked to hear how frequently Beth had visited Bathington. No one in Sleighville had known, otherwise they would've mentioned it when he interviewed them. But to be fair, Beth hadn't been close to anyone in town. As Nick had described her, she'd been closed-off and kept to herself, even with her siblings.

Then he left without checking on Noel. Not that Nick would've let him. His expression had given off stay away vibes, as if he'd hurt her or something. Make her cry. He was pissed but not upset enough to knock her down when she was already lying on the floor.

His fist connected with the door. If he didn't do it now, he never would.

Eve opened the door. She knew right away something was wrong.

"I'll get Griffin. Go take a seat in the living room."

Griffin met him less than a minute later, taking a seat next to him. "What's wrong?"

Instead of answering with words, he pulled out his phone, went to his email, and played the video.

Griffin grabbed his phone. "Where did you get this?"

Duke huffed a long sigh. "That's a very long story."

His boss—and best friend—looked at him with patience Duke didn't feel. Griffin would wait him out.

So he spilled it all. Most of everything Nick told him. What happened to Noel, though he needed a better description of what actually happened to her tonight. Especially if he wanted to find the bastard who dared to put a hand on her.

Hell, he even admitted to sleeping with her. He let Griffin assume it was the one time. At his house. Since everyone knew she came alone without her brother.

Then he leaned back into the couch.

"I'm an idiot."

Griffin relaxed next to him. "You're not. You did your best with the information you had."

Maybe.

But not entirely what he was talking about.

He let himself get played. Used like he meant nothing.

Even casual sex should have a modicum of respect. Noel had shown she had none for him.

Walter strolled into the room and jumped up on Griffin's

lap, nudging his hand for a rub. Griffin obliged him. His low purring soothed the torment he felt building inside.

"How do you think Warren Benson knew Beth?"

Griffin shook his head. "That's a very good question. That man is a hermit. He never leaves his house."

Which made his visit to Rosetta's even more curious. He lived just outside of town. Deep in the woods all by himself. Warren was Gerald, Juliet's ex-husband's grandfather. Gerald was doing ten years in prison for abusing Juliet. He had eight and half years to go. But even before he got locked up, he rarely saw his grandfather. Gregory, Warren's other grandson, as far as Duke knew, didn't visit the old man either. Their father, Wesley, hadn't been seen in town for years. He'd left one day and never returned. Duke wasn't sure if Gregory even knew where his father was.

He'd be visiting Gregory as well.

"I was going to head there tonight. I want answers."

Griffin let Walter jump down before standing up. "Let me change. I'll go with you."

"I need to swing by my house and change as well." They both had to knock on the door in official capacity.

He waited by the door while Griffin got ready. Eve met him. "Griffin gave me a rushed version. I'll go check on Noel while you're gone."

"Try and get her to go to the hospital. It looks like whoever hit her, hit her hard in the head."

Eve touched his shoulder. "I will."

Then they left. The stop at his house was quick. By the time they pulled into Warren's driveway, Duke's anger had risen again. He knew the old man couldn't have killed Beth, or even hurt Noel. He was in his eighties and had a hard time walking. He didn't have the strength anymore to hurt someone. But he had to know who did.

Griffin knocked on the door while Duke stood to the side with his hand on the butt of his gun. Looking casual, but his body was tense and ready for anything.

Warren didn't greet them with a pleasant expression. "Yeah?"

"Can we come in and talk, Warren?" Griffin asked in his nice friendly chief of police voice. When dealing with the gruff old man, one had to keep their cool. Otherwise he'd clam up and they'd never get any answers.

"No. Say your piece right there."

Griffin pulled out his phone, showing Warren the video of him arguing with Beth. "I know you know Beth Terden. I know you had to have heard her body was found in Tinsel Lake. So what I want to know is what this conversation was about? It happened a week before she disappeared."

Warren looked from Griffin to him, then back to Griffin. "Not your concern. I said my piece to the girl and that was that."

Not good enough.

"We need to know what it was about." Duke pointed at the phone. "Because that wasn't you saying your piece. That was you hollering and spitting into the face of a young girl who was minding her own business."

Warren took a step outside the doorway, causing them to back up a step. "Minding her own business? That girl was a damn nuisance! Coming onto my property all the time. Knocking on my damn door. She never minded my business, so I returned the favor."

"Why was she bothering you, Warren?" Griffin asked, not appearing affected by his outburst at all. Though Duke knew he was ready for anything. "You could've come to the police department and filed a complaint."

"Bah! I can handle a stupid little girl."

"Did you handle her a little too roughly?" Duke asked. Might as well get the question out of the way. Though he doubted he strangled her.

"I can barely open a jar of pickles on a good day. You think I could wrap my hands around that girl's neck and squeeze? Bah!"

"Why was she bothering you, Warren?" Griffin asked again.

"That was between me and her. We settled it that night, and she never bothered me again."

"Because she was strangled and dumped into a lake, Warren," Duke said through gritted teeth.

"I don't have to tell you shit. Now get off my property."

Then he hobbled backward a few steps and slammed the door.

"Maybe his grandson knows."

They left and knocked on Gregory's door. He answered nearly identical to his grandfather.

"Yes?"

And Griffin started out the conversation as he had with Warren. "Can we come in and talk?"

Despite Gregory hating Griffin's guts, since Griffin's sister put his brother in jail, he let them inside.

"We had a chat with your grandfather. He wasn't very open with us. We're hoping you can help fill in some of the blanks."

Gregory looked guarded. Though, Duke always thought he looked that way. Ever since his brother had been locked up, he'd changed. Not that he'd ever liked the Benson's, even before Gerald married Juliet.

"I doubt it. I haven't seen him in a long time. He keeps to himself."

Griffin showed Gregory the video of his grandfather and Beth arguing.

"Well, I didn't see that coming."

"So you don't know how your grandfather knew Beth?" Duke asked.

With Gregory's shields up, he couldn't quite tell if he was lying or not.

"I had no idea."

"He won't tell us what they were arguing about," Griffin added.

Gregory shrugged, laughing. "If I had no idea they knew each other, how would I know what they were arguing about? I'm sorry I can't help you." More laughter came out. "Wow, you lock up my brother and now you're trying to lock up my grandfather for murder. Like he could actually strangle somebody."

Griffin tensed next to him. "Your brother beat my sister. He committed a crime. That's why he got locked up."

"She's a liar!"

"Oh, so she beat herself, did she?" Griffin spat back.

Okay. This situation was turning sour real quick.

Duke stepped in front of Griffin. "We're done arguing. Talk with your grandfather and see if he'll tell you what they argued about. Let me know."

Gregory crossed his arms, his mouth twisted in disgust. "What makes you think I want to help you pigs out? Throw another member of my family in prison?"

"I don't think your grandfather killed Beth." Or hurt Noel, not that he'd mention her attack to this asshole. Especially if he, by some chance, had been the one to do it. That would tip his hand Noel had gone to the police. "But he could point us in the right direction. Stop lying to yourself, Gregory. You're not doing yourself any favors pretending like your brother was a saint. Or your grandfather."

Because the whole town knew Warren beat his son. No doubt his son beat his two boys. Which was why Gerald had beaten Juliet. Like grandfather, like son, like grandson. It was too bad Juliet hadn't realized what fate she had fallen into. Not that Duke was blaming her for marrying the man. He had been a charming individual. No one had thought he'd hurt her.

They left, with Duke practically pushing Griffin out of the house.

"That asshole..." Griffin gripped the steering wheel.

"He was trying to piss you off. We should've known he wouldn't help us." Duke buckled his belt. "We'll find what we're looking for."

Because he wouldn't have it any other way. He'd sworn to Beth—not alive, of course—that he'd find her killer, and he wouldn't break his word.

Noel woke up on her own, for the first time the entire night. She vaguely remembered Eve stopping by and telling her brother she should go to the hospital. She remembered going hysterical hearing that and her brother calming her down in the usual way he did. Then Eve saying he needed to watch signs for a concussion at the very least. Which was why she'd been woken up every hour on the hour. At one point in the middle of the night, she remembered his frantic worry and him picking her up until she responded. He'd been ready to bring her to the hospital.

Her head hurt. Like someone had drilled a bunch of nails deep into her skull. But she was fine. It would eventually go away. Maybe she had a small concussion, but she survived the night and her bruises and scrapes would heal. No need for the sterile environment that would bring back painful memories best forgotten.

She used the bathroom, showering, letting the hot water hit her until the water started turning cold. The clothes she put on didn't match and she didn't care. Like the day her brother had breakfast on the table waiting for her, he had done it again.

What would she do without him? Always taking care of her.

She'd come to this town thinking she could do all this on her own. What a lie she had told herself. She never would've gotten very far if her brother hadn't come with her.

"Go on. Eat. You need it."

She sat down, munching on the food, but not digesting a whole lot of it.

"More, Noel. You need to keep up your strength. You can't go back into the depression like you did a few weeks ago."

When he'd told her Beth had been killed.

Yeah, she had stopped living for a whole week. Not eating. Not sleeping. Not caring about anything but imagining what her sister must've endured.

Nick was right.

She couldn't do that to herself. In the last few days, since seeing her brutalized body on the wall, she had reverted back to the horror of herself. She had to be strong for Beth. To find this killer.

The food disappeared until the plate was clear.

"Much better." Nick took her plate and brought it to the sink. She heard him sigh before he turned around. "I think it's time we go back home."

"But Beth—"

"I told Duke everything we know last night. It's his job to find her killer, and I think we let him do that."

She crossed her arms and pouted. "You're saying that because I got hurt."

"Yes! Noel, you could've died!" Nick ran his hands through his hair, pulling on the ends. "I can't lose you too. Okay. We're leaving. I'm taking a shower and we're packing up."

He walked past her and she couldn't help herself.

"Enjoy your shower."

"I will, brat! I know you used up the hot water." His voice echoed from the hallway.

She wasn't ready to leave.

Not like this.

They were so close.

She was about to sit on the couch when the doorbell rang. A glance through the peephole had her thinking she should go back and hide in her room.

But she had decided she couldn't act that way anymore. She couldn't let the fear take control.

She opened the door.

Duke didn't smile, but he also didn't look angry.

"Come in."

She walked away and took a seat on the couch, curling her legs underneath her. Duke closed the door, looking around the room.

"Where's your brother?"

His aloof expression turned into worry in a split second. Huh. So maybe he didn't hate her if he worried she'd been left alone.

"In the shower."

The concern evaporated. Though he still looked tense as

he took a seat. The couch was small, so it put him closer to her than he wanted. He could've remained standing then. It was his own fault.

"How are you?"

"Fine."

He frowned. "You look better. You didn't go get checked out. You should."

"It's just a few bruises. I'm fine."

She would never step inside a hospital unless she was dying. Even then, death would be welcome.

"I need to ask you some questions, Noel."

About all her lying. Yeah, not something she wanted to discuss. Maybe it was best they were leaving town sooner rather than later.

"I know you don't want to revisit it, but I need to know more about what happened to you."

Oh. He meant what happened last night.

"I didn't see his face. Or recognize his voice. He whispered, so it was hard to make it out."

"It's okay. Walk me through what happened."

She looked away, unable to meet his eyes. He was keeping this visit professional, then so would she. "I had to park far away from the cafe because there were no spots in front of it. I had to cut through an alley. I wasn't paying attention. My mind had wandered. One second I was walking, then I was being slammed against the brick wall. I had no time to fight back." And she should've fought back. She'd trained to defend herself. To prevent this very thing from happening.

She shuddered, remembering the way it felt to hit the wall. It brought back memories of the other times she'd been hit by a fist. The sound of a fist hitting bone. The blood filling her mouth. The pain that echoed all over her body.

"Hey," Duke soothed, scooting closer to her, brushing his hand against her cheek. "It's okay. We can do this later."

She closed her eyes, savoring his delicate touch. It would be the last time he ever did so.

They couldn't do this later.

They were leaving town.

Her eyes opened to see the concern back in his eyes. His hand dropped from her cheek and she missed the warmth of his touch.

"He came up behind me. He twisted my arm so fast, I had no time to react. Then his hand was on my neck, squeezing hard. I couldn't breathe."

That was the nice thing about her father. He was predicable in his beatings. He used his fists, making contact in the face and stomach. On occasion, when he knocked them to the floor, he'd use his boot to kick them as well. But he never used an open hand. He never grabbed them around the neck and restricted their air. It had been a new sensation, and it had frightened her more than anything else she'd ever experienced.

"He whispered in my ear to stop looking into Beth's case. He squeezed my neck harder. Then he told me if I didn't, I'd be next. Then he slammed my head into the wall again and I don't remember anything after that. I remember waking up alone in the alley."

"He knocked you out." Duke's hands fisted in his lap, then he relaxed his body. "You were very lucky he didn't do anything else."

"I know." She wrapped her arms around herself, knowing how true that was.

"I already checked out the security cameras around the area and I didn't see anything. Not anything that stood out anyway. There are no cameras in the alley."

"How did you know where to look?"

He grinned, displaying his delectable dimples. She soaked up the beautiful expression, thinking she'd never see it again from him. His two sweet dimples. "Nick told me you went to get food. I searched the area and found your bag of food. It didn't take much detective skills on my part."

Then he lost the grin. "I failed your sister. I should have been more diligent in my search. Because if I had, I would've found she argued with Warren, and you would've never been put in the middle."

"No, Duke." She reached out to touch him but stopped herself. He wouldn't want her touching him. He hated her. He had to. "You can't blame yourself. You did what you could. You haven't given up. The room at your house is proof of that. I appreciate it. So don't blame yourself." Then she ran his words through her head again. "Wait? Warren? You found out who that man is." If he had told Nick, her brother hadn't relayed the news.

"I recognized him right away. He lives in town. Well, on the outskirts of town. He's a recluse. Doesn't leave his house much. Doesn't get along with many people. I was surprised to see he even left his house to go argue with Beth."

"We need to go talk to him." She perked up.

Duke laid a hand on her knee. "*You* need to stay out of this. I already talked to him."

"What did he say?"

The look he gave her said he couldn't believe she asked the question. As if she didn't have a right to know.

"She was my sister. I deserve to know."

"He didn't tell us. He's an asshole. Could be because of that. Could be because Juliet was married to his grandson Gerald, and well, Gerald hurt her and is sitting in prison because of it. Bad blood between the Stuarts and that family."

She knew she should be paying attention, but Duke's hand was still on her knee. His thumb was moving in a slow motion, igniting her senses. His touch always did that to her.

"You have to let me handle this, Noel. I can't see—" He swallowed hard, his hand putting pressure on her knee. "I can't see you hurt again like that." His eyes zeroed in on the bruise on her neck. "I hate seeing those marks on your body."

And he hated her.

"No." He leaned closer, moving his hand from her knee and cupping the back of her head. "No, I don't hate you."

Oh, she had said that out loud.

"I should though. I should hate you."

12

NOEL FLINCHED. He knew he'd made another wrong move, saying the wrong thing. But it was true. If they were going to move past this, they had to start being honest with each other.

"You used me."

Her hands reached out, clutching his shirt. "I didn't. What happened between us just happened. I didn't plan any of that. It's not as if I ever brought up Beth. If I had used you, I would've tried to get information out of you. But did I? Did I do that?"

She had a point.

He rubbed his hand behind her head. Her eyes dilated in pleasure at his touch.

"Well, you lied to me."

She unclenched her hands, letting go of his shirt. But she didn't move her hands from his chest. "I will admit to that. I didn't tell you the whole truth of why we were here. Nick didn't come along to the fish fry, not because of stomach issues, but because he was digging into the case. So yeah, you got me there. I lied. I'm sorry. I'm truly sorry, Duke. I never meant to lie to you."

He rested his forehead gently against hers. "What am I going to do with you, Noel? I want to stay mad and yet, I want to kiss you so badly I can't stand it."

The war he'd been raging with himself all night and into the morning had caused him to get a headache. Then it brought him to her doorstep.

As much as he wanted to stay mad at her, he didn't think he could.

"Duke..." she whispered breathlessly.

Oh, yeah. He wouldn't be able to resist the temptation in his arms.

Then a throat cleared.

Duke backed away from Noel, letting his hand drop away. He even stood up from the couch when he saw Nick's expression. A mixture of confusion and fury.

"Someone want to tell me what's going on? You were a little too close to my sister."

"Just making sure she was okay from yesterday."

"Yeah, that doesn't require you to get damn near mouth to mouth with her. Like you were about to kiss her."

Noel scrambled from the couch and got between them. Nick had advanced toward him.

"Stop. Everything's fine."

"That didn't look fine to me."

Duke couldn't see her face, but he knew she was struggling. A lie was on the tip of her tongue. While he didn't want more lies between them—that included with her brother—he was willing to let this one slide. Anything to avoid a physical altercation with the guy.

"I don't want to leave, Nick."

"What?" Nick sounded confused at the abrupt conversation change. "Tough shit."

They were leaving? How soon?

Did it matter?

That was a very good idea. The farther away she was from this killer, the better.

"I don't know when you two planned to leave, but that's a good idea."

Noel shifted her stance so he could see the betrayal on her face. As if he'd done something wrong. Of course he'd said the wrong thing again. That's all he did with her—do or say the wrong thing.

"No, I'm not leaving yet."

"Sis, we ain't arguing about this," Nick growled with frustration.

"I will stay out of the way with Beth's case." She glanced at them to make sure they heard her. It had been loud and clear. There was no way to misinterpret it. "But I can't leave until things are settled between Duke and I."

Nick's fury reanimated into his features. "What the hell does that mean?"

"Nick, did you ever wonder why I went to Duke first last night before you?"

He shrugged. "Because he's a police officer."

"Yeah, partly. I was on autopilot driving. I surprised even myself when I ended up at his house and not here. But I think it's because I always feel safe and secure in his arms." She grabbed her brother's arm, and Duke didn't think it was to hold him in place. "Not that I don't feel safe with you. It's a different feeling I get with Duke, and I needed that so badly last night. I needed him to hold me for a second. I can't leave yet. He hates me, and I can't leave when he hates me."

Her voice had wobbled at the end. He heard the tears as she ran out of the room.

Duke looked at Nick. He stood in his way to get to Noel. Of course, he had to follow her to tell her once again he didn't hate her.

"I need you tell me what the hell happened that night when you were alone with my sister. Now."

There was no avoiding this. Why keep it a secret any longer? Why did it matter?

"She's a grown woman who can make her own decisions. You have no right to get mad if we slept together."

And that was the damn truth. Brother or not, it wasn't his business. Of course, he was an only child and didn't know what it was like having a sister and worrying about her. So who was he to tell Nick how to feel.

"My sister is fragile right now. She's vulnerable. She's not in the right frame of mind to be starting a relationship."

It never was a relationship. Though Duke was smart enough not to say that.

"I don't believe that. I think she's stronger than we both realize." Duke loosened his stance, not wanting to give off fight-me vibes. "I don't want to do this with you, Nick. I don't want to be at odds with each other. You're right. I could arrest you for hacking into Rosetta's. You can thank your sister for that. I don't think I could bear to devastate her by arresting you. I know why you hacked into the system. To find answers that I couldn't find. I would never hurt her. And I don't hate her. I can't. It's impossible to hate someone so sweet and vibrant and who makes me laugh in a way I haven't in a long time."

Nick stepped to the side, sweeping his hands for Duke to pass. "Make peace then so we can leave. Clearly she won't until you do."

Except he didn't want them to leave. He wasn't ready to let her go yet.

He moved past Nick and down the short hallway. The door was open, so he peeked his head in. He didn't bother asking for an invitation. Hell, it was probably the wrong move, but he did it anyway.

He climbed onto the bed and wrapped his arms around her, pulling her back snug against his chest. Her tears were quiet, but he knew she was still crying.

"You know I don't hate you. I already told you that," he whispered, kissing the back of her head.

"I know. I hate myself for hurting you."

"Please don't. I'm not mad anymore."

She half-sniffled, half-laughed. "That fast, uh?"

"If it gets you to stop crying, yes. I can't stand to hear your tears. No hate is allowed between us. That includes toward yourself." His lips pressed against her hair again. "You should leave, Noel. It's safer."

"I'm not ready." She covered his arms with her own, trapping them together. "Hold me, Duke. That's all I want right now. I want to forget everything but how I feel in your arms."

So he obliged her request. He held her. Didn't speak. Didn't move. Didn't even kiss her head like he wanted to one more time.

He just held her.

SHE STROLLED into the kitchen feeling like a zombie. Her hair was all over the place. While she hadn't looked in the mirror, she knew there would be dark circles under her eyes. The pounding in her head she'd had all day yesterday was still there, though a dull ache now. As long as she didn't go into another bout of tears, it would be gone in a few hours after she took some medication.

"Where's my breakfast? You always have my breakfast ready."

Nick turned away from the coffee pot, blowing on the top of the mug before taking a sip. "First shower, then your food will magically appear."

She would shower. Eventually.

Yesterday had been exhausting and her emotions had been all over the place. Duke had held her in his arms for the longest time. She wasn't sure how long. She'd fallen asleep. By the time she awoke, it had been evening, and Duke had been gone. Nick made her supper, though they didn't talk much. She didn't ask when Duke had left, and how long he had stayed. After eating, she returned to the bedroom and went right back to bed. But not before crying one more time.

Well, she was done crying.

Done wallowing in her grief. In her guilt that she had somehow failed her sister.

Acting the way she had wouldn't bring Beth justice. It didn't solve any problems. So she had to pull herself out of it.

"I'm not leaving yet, Nick."

He hadn't forced her to vacate the cottage yesterday, but she knew he would today. She was putting her foot down.

"You spent all afternoon with Duke. Things have to be settled." He took a sip of coffee. "While he's not arresting me for what I did, I hate to push my luck with the guy."

She didn't even think about that part. But if Duke had any intention of doing that, he would've already. She crossed her arms. "Well, things aren't settled. I fell asleep."

He gazed down at his coffee mug. "Yeah, I know. I monitored the situation the whole time."

An annoyed laugh escaped as she shook her head. "Of course you did. And what did Duke have to say about that?"

"We didn't chat. For a while, he fell asleep too."

Nick sipped his coffee.

"I can't leave, and not just because of Duke. Because of Beth. It feels unfinished, and I can't leave."

He sighed. "I won't risk your life."

"I won't allow that to happen again. I was distracted. I couldn't get the images of her body out of my head. Tactical error on my part."

"And what? You've magically gotten those images out of your head? I doubt it. I know you, Noel. Better than you know yourself."

She didn't want to argue that point as it might be true. He'd taken care of her for so long, he did know her well.

"I need to do this my way. I can't keep crying. I can't keep letting my fear win." She refused to let it win. "I don't know if we need a membership here or what, but I'm going to the gym and I have to work out. I have to exercise the demons trying to take a hold of me."

He looked at her for the longest time, then set his coffee mug down. "Which means you need someone to spar with."

She grinned.

"Damn it. Just don't break any of my bones, okay?"

Her fingers drew a cross over her heart. "Promise."

"Then let's go."

Her brother knew she wouldn't take a shower yet because they were about to work up a sweat. And she didn't like to eat—especially a hearty meal like he made—before working out.

They both changed and left for the gym. It was a nice

facility off the main street in town. The mixture of Halloween and Christmas decorations outside the building made her giggle, lifting her spirits. Skeletons wearing Santa hats. Rudolph pulling a wagon with hay on it, with a masked skeleton holding a chain saw riding the wagon. She loved the creativity around town. Though, it was time to take that stuff down as Halloween was over. She wanted to see turkeys gathered around. They couldn't forget about Thanksgiving.

They weren't required to sign up for a membership, but they had to pay a small fee to use the facility. No problem. Anything to get inside and start working out.

She never went anywhere without her equipment, so she had her boxing gloves and mouthguard handy. As did Nick, because he knew her well, knowing this might happen.

Then they started. Her attacking and him on the receiving end. Taking blows and letting her have the control. Though, she was much better at kickboxing than he was, so it wasn't as if he was *letting* her win or anything.

It didn't take long to work up a sweat. They went at it for a good half hour before taking a small break to get some water. Nothing else. Then they were right back at it. She'd gotten a few decent punches at him, one connecting with his face a little too hard. Nick didn't do anything but get back on his feet and resume position. Every time she threw a punch or delivered a well-placed kick, she felt lighter inside. She imagined the unknown man who had attacked her and that he was the one in front of her. It made her punches more impactful, her kicks that much more intense.

Her last kick was a hard-delivered roundhouse kick, hitting Nick square in the ribs, dropping him to the floor.

He groaned, holding his side. "Shit, Noel. We done yet? I think you cracked a rib."

She bounced on her feet, laughing. "I didn't. Don't be a baby."

He used his gloved hand to push himself up and off the ground, still holding his side. "No, seriously, it feels like you cracked a rib."

She stopped moving, letting her arms drop to her sides. "I would know if I cracked your rib. I didn't."

"It's my rib. How would you know?"

She shrugged, unable to hide a wicked grin. "I just do."

"Okay, fine. It's severely bruised. I hurt. I need a break."

Well, they had been at it for a long time. At least an hour. For the first time exercising in this manner in quite a few weeks, it was a good start. She hadn't been to the gym since Nick had told her the news about Beth. That had been a huge error on her part. She should've hit the ring right away. She should have never let her grief consume her as she had.

While Sleighville didn't have a boxing ring, the small area with the mats to help lessen the blows worked fine. Because Nick managed to knock her down a time or two. But not as much as she did to him.

"Wuss. If you can't handle it, we'll take a break."

Nick laughed, then groaned, telling her that maybe she had hurt him more than she intended. "I like seeing you laugh again and being more yourself. We can go again later."

That's one of the reasons she loved her brother so much. His willingness to do anything for her.

A quiet clapping had them turning toward the entrance to the small room they were in. The chief of police even whistled. "That was impressive. Duke told me

Nick had said you could dropkick his ass. You weren't lying about it."

"Contrary to what has happened, we haven't lied to anyone here. We just didn't tell you everything." Nick held his left side while he took a drink of water after pulling off his gloves.

Griffin mulled that over, pursing his lips and scrunching his brows. "Semantics. Still sort of lying, but that's not why I'm here."

Noel pulled her gloves off, deciding she'd let Nick take the lead. For now. She wasn't sure she wanted to know why the chief of police was here.

"What can we help you with, Chief?"

"It's Griffin. I insist you call me Griffin. I did have you over at my house to share a meal."

"Okay, *Griffin*," Nick emphasized, "How can we help you?"

"I wanted to express my condolences about your sister. I didn't know Beth well." The frown still marred his face. "I didn't go out of my way to know her. I was friendly with her, as I am with most of the townsfolk. But it pains me that we all thought she up and left. That we didn't take her disappearance as a serious matter. I'm sorry what happened to her. Duke mentioned you're leaving. I wanted to make sure I told you how sorry I am before you do. I noticed your car was gone in the driveway this morning and I was afraid I was too late."

She wanted to get right back to the kickboxing. She could feel the grief resurfacing. Or maybe it was the kindness she heard in his voice, as if he were truly sorry. That was hard to hear.

"Thank you. Appreciate it. It wasn't your fault. Beth could be aloof and closed-off, even with us. And we knew her for the past fourteen years. So don't feel bad you thought she left town on her own accord. She left us without a word goodbye."

"I promise you we will try our best to find who killed her. I will keep you updated if we do."

She noticed he didn't promise them that he would find her killer, but that he would try. While she hated the choice of words, she appreciated he didn't give them false hope. That he knew it might be impossible to find who did it.

"So that Warren dude was a complete dead-end?" Nick asked.

Griffin winced. "For now. He won't tell us what they argued about."

"Because there's bad blood between your families?" Noel finally spoke, remembering what Duke had said.

"Unfortunately, yeah. My sister was married to his grandson. She hid the abuse for way too long. It kills me she did. But he's where he belongs now. But even without that, Warren has always kept to himself, and very uncooperative in most things."

"I'd like to talk to him."

Nick snapped his attention at her. "I don't think so."

She glanced from her brother to Griffin. "We came here to find Beth's killer. I already told you I'm not leaving until this is settled. It's not settled. We found that lead, and I want to follow up on it. I didn't say I would go alone. Feel free to come with. I doubt an eighty-year-old man attacked me or Beth, but I want to know why they were arguing."

"Fine. You don't go without me."

Griffin cleared his throat. "Or me."

Noel gave him a serene smile. "Griffin, I don't think that's a great idea. He's less likely to talk to me with you there."

"I'll stay in the car," Griffin replied, "but I don't feel

comfortable you two going there by yourself. Not that I think you can't handle yourself." He waved a hand at the mat. "Because clearly you can. He's unpredictable though, and I'd feel better going along."

She and Nick shared a long look. "Okay, fine. But you both stay in the car. I'll have a better chance on my own."

Neither looked like they enjoyed that idea, but they also didn't argue with her about it.

It was time to get some answers.

She wouldn't leave that old man's house until she did.

13

NOEL CONVINCED Griffin that it would be wiser to take their rental car to Warren's house. If he saw signs the chief of police was with, he'd clam up. Nick drove with her in the front passenger seat while Griffin sat in the back. He also wasn't in uniform. So if Warren did notice him in the vehicle, he would know Griffin hadn't come in the official capacity. At least, she hoped he thought that.

"Promise me you'll stay in the car."

Nick gripped the steering wheel. "I promise I'll stay in the car...as long as it all looks fine. One thing makes me nervous and I'm by your side. It's non-negotiable."

She'd take it because there would be no arguing about it. They would only go in circles.

Her body protested exiting the car. It hadn't seen the kind of exercise she'd done today in weeks. She needed to build her stamina back up.

They'd left the gym and gone back to the cottage, showering, eating, and getting ready before leaving for Warren's. Griffin met them an hour later in their driveway to leave.

Now the moment was upon her.

What would she find out?

The door opened before she could knock. The old man looked tired but alert.

"Get off my property. Take the damn chief of police and whoever else is in the car with you."

Well, he had decent eyesight if he already noticed Griffin in the car.

"That's a rude way to greet someone."

He flinched—subtle, but enough she noticed it—as if he were surprised by her response. As if because she was a woman she'd be frightened by him.

"I'm Beth Terden's sister." Half-sister, but she didn't think that part mattered because she was her whole sister in every sense. "I want answers. If you think posturing and using a tough, mean voice is going to get me off this porch, you're wrong."

Warren's eyes narrowed into tiny slits, assessing her. "Then come in. Say your piece and get off my property."

He walked away from the door. She glanced back at the car, holding her hand down to tell them to hold back, give her this opportunity. Then she stepped inside and shut the door. Without seeing the look on her brother's face, she knew he exploded with fury and irritation that she'd entered the wolves' den. Maybe that's why Warren invited her in. To upset the men in the car. To throw everyone off-balance.

Warren took a seat on an old recliner that creaked as he sat down. She sat on the couch near him.

"What did you and my sister argue about?"

"I tell you and you'll never bother me again? Because I told that girl something she didn't want to hear and she kept coming back like I was lying."

"I will leave and never come back if you tell me the truth."

"Ain't no reason for me to lie."

"Okay, so tell me what you and my sister argued about."

He settled into his seat. "She came knocking on my door telling me some nonsense that I was her grandfather. I told her she was mistaken and to get off my property. She kept coming back over and over telling me I was wrong. The last time she came here, I wasn't home. She left a damn letter giving me some sob story. I had enough. So I tracked her down and told her to her face *in her territory* that enough was enough. I think I got through to her because I never saw her again. End of story."

"You never saw her again because someone killed her."

He flinched again, but didn't say anything.

"Why did she think you were her grandfather?"

Because as far as Noel knew, she had no other family. When Beth appeared on their doorstep, she had said her mom died and she had no one left. She never talked about anyone else on her mom's side of the family.

"Some nonsense about a daughter I don't have. I have one son. One child. Wesley. He's a real son of a bitch."

No surprise there with how he acted. Like father, like son.

"And she didn't believe you?"

"You daft? What part of my explanation didn't you understand?"

Right. Of course, Beth didn't believe him because she kept coming back.

"I guess I don't understand the part where she insisted you were if you don't have a daughter."

Beth rarely talked about her mother, so Noel didn't know much about her. Noel never pried because she understood the importance of keeping some things to yourself. She never talked about her family either. How her mom gave up on life. How her father abused them until the day he died. How the only person she could ever count on was her brother. None of that was easy to talk about.

He shrugged. "I don't know what was going on in that crazy mind of hers."

Noel leaned forward, pointing a sharp finger at him. "My sister wasn't crazy. Watch your mouth."

The old man chuckled. "You are so unalike. She was very timid every time she came. You can't hold your tongue."

"No, I never could hold my tongue to assholes."

More evil laughter filled the space. "She had some *crazy* story that her mother was a daughter I never knew."

Noel gritted her teeth hearing the word crazy again. "So you cheated on your wife."

"I held my wedding vows until the day my pretty wife died."

The sinister look in his eyes had a sickening feeling erupting in her gut. "Thank you for your time. And the truth. I don't know why my sister bothered to insist you were her grandfather. You didn't deserve to even breathe the same air as her. She deserved someone better than you as potential family."

One thing Noel knew was Beth was always searching for more family. For a piece of her to belong somewhere. Noel had struggled at times wondering why her and Nick were never good enough for Beth. They had been her family. But she had also never stopped her sister from looking. She'd found a lead and left without telling her because she must've thought Noel wouldn't support her. Oh, how wrong she'd been. Noel would've supported her in every single way.

Noel stood up. Warren did as well, more agile on his feet than she thought. Until he wobbled.

"Now don't come back."

"I won't." Noel headed for the door, stopping a few feet away from it. "Do you still have the letter she gave you?"

Warren's beady eyes stared hard at her. "Why? You want it?"

"Well, I'm not going to beg on my knees, but yes, for once in your miserable life, you could do a nice deed and give it to me."

The old man chuckled, then walked to a desk by the wall, digging in the drawer. He walked toward her, careful with his steps. "I bet your father had to beat a lot of sense into you and how to act like a docile woman."

She snatched the letter from his hand. "I guess he didn't beat me hard enough."

Warren's laughter rang in her ears as she exited his house, slamming the door on the way out.

She was shaking by the time she returned to the car.

"What happened? Did he touch you?" Nick demanded, seeing her agitation.

"He's a horrible man. He's pure evil."

And yet, he'd given her the truth and the letter without much arguing.

"I'll repeat Nick's question. Did he touch you?"

She swirled her attention to the back seat, noticing Griffin had his hand on the doorhandle, ready to exit and arrest a cranky old man.

"No. No, he didn't. But he gave me answers. Some that make sense. Some that don't."

She held up the letter. The first piece of evidence. But would it lead to the killer?

DEAR MR. BENSON,

I know you don't like me stopping by your place all the time, and I want to say I'm sorry. I am. But I can't help it. You never want to listen to what I have to say, so you will listen now. My mother had a hard life. Trying to provide for me. Trying to make ends meet. She never talked about my dad. No matter how many times I asked about him, she would just tell me he was dead. So I would switch gears and ask about my grandparents. She would never talk about them either. They were dead too. Everyone was apparently dead to her. I hated that. I wanted more than just a mom, even if she did love me as much as she could. But if she loved me as much as she said she did, she would've given me more of a family. I found my father after my mom died. Turned out he was dead. Just like she said. Of course when she said it, he wasn't dead yet. I have two siblings. One brother and one sister. While I love that they accepted me into their life, I still feel like something is missing. A part of me is missing. So I kept looking and searching until I came across you. It wasn't easy. It caused many tearful nights for myself. But I found you. You can deny all you want that I'm not your granddaughter, but it doesn't change the fact you are. I'm not asking for money or anything else. I'm asking for you to hear me out and let me be a part of your family. What is so wrong in that? You seem lonely out here in the woods. I feel lonely at times too. So let's be lonely together. I want to know more of my family. I don't think that's asking a whole lot. Thanks for hearing me out for once. Of course I didn't give you a choice, unless of course, you threw this away before reading it. I'm going to pretend you are reading it though.

With love,

Beth Terden, your granddaughter

DUKE RACED over to Griffin's the minute he called telling him about the visit to Warren. After reading the letter Warren had given Noel, he was confused more than ever. This was all about a long-lost granddaughter.

He looked at Griffin as they stood in the living room. Nick was lounging on the couch. He wasn't sure where Noel was at, but considering Eve wasn't in the room either, he figured they were somewhere together in the house.

"I first want to say I don't like the fact Noel went inside that house alone."

Griffin had the decency to look chagrined. Nick smirked, shaking his head, as if Duke didn't know what he was talking about.

"It was the wrong move."

"It got us that letter and more answers than you two got," Nick retorted.

It did, but Duke didn't like the thought of her in danger. That old man was unpredictable. Always had been.

"His wife died when their son was five years old. She drowned in the lake behind the house. The chief of police at the time could never prove he did it, but it was always suspected that he had." Duke looked at Nick as he told the story since he didn't know the history. "She couldn't swim, so it was reasonable she had drowned. But because she couldn't swim, she never went near the lake. So how did she die by drowning?"

"He told Noel that he held his wedding vows until the day his wife died," Griffin pointed out. "That doesn't mean he didn't have a daughter with another woman. Beth could have been right about it all."

Nick pushed himself off the couch and joined the

conversation on his feet. "Okay, so this old guy could be her grandfather. How does that translate into her getting killed?"

"We need to talk to Gregory again." Duke shared a look with Griffin. "Ask him if Beth ever approached him about this. It would make them half-cousins." Duke looked at Nick. "It sounds like, based off the letter, she would've liked to get to know more family."

Nick crossed his arms, giving a short nod. "I believe that. What's this Gregory like? Would he have hurt Beth?"

Duke and Griffin shared another look. They said in unison, "Yeah."

Nick laughed. "So why are you two still standing here?"

Griffin blew out a breath, running a hand through his hair. "I'm afraid he's not going to be responsive to us. Maybe it's time we call in some help. Have someone else interview him."

Duke knew Griffin wasn't wrong, but he hated the thought of handing it off to someone else.

"I'll do it."

Duke pierced Nick with a stern look. "I don't think so. You're not law enforcement." And he'd already messed in things he shouldn't have.

"Yeah, but we might've shared family. I mean, I'm not related to this asshole, but Beth was and she was my family. We're connected in a way. I don't have to be as diplomatic as you two."

Griffin grinned, laughing. "He's not wrong."

Well, at least it wasn't Noel offering to do it, because that would've been a big hell no. Duke was still irritated at what they let her do with Warren.

"Okay, but we'll hang back in the car. If things go sideways."

"Whatever. If you want. Tell me everything you already asked him about Beth. Recently and in the past."

So Duke and Griffin did just that. They let Nick know that Gregory claimed not to have known how his grandfather knew Beth. He could've been lying, which Duke was leaning toward he was. Because if Beth approached Warren, it stood to reason she approached Gregory too.

When they first found her body, Duke interviewed most people, including Gregory. He claimed the only time he ever interacted with her was in the cafe while working. Duke, at the time, had no reason to doubt that. It had been what most people had said. It seemed reasonable. Though, Gregory didn't venture into the cafe often, not with the bad blood between his family and Juliet.

"Let me tell Noel I'm leaving. I'll meet you outside." Nick walked out of the living room.

Duke wanted to follow. To see Noel. To check on her. To hold her again.

Leaving last night had been one of the hardest things to do, especially while she'd been sleeping. But every time Nick peeked into the room, he felt his irritation that he was laying with his sister. He didn't want to antagonize the man or cause problems, so he left. At the time, it had been a good decision.

When he got home to his quiet, dark house, he regretted it. He wanted to be back in that bed, holding Noel as close as he could.

The entire morning, he waged another battle with himself on dropping by the cottage. Or even sending her a text.

He should still be mad at her for her deception. Yet, he wasn't. The moment he entered that room and laid down with her, it had evaporated. He'd forgiven her for the few lies she had told. It was impossible to stay mad at her when he understood the reasoning behind it all. She had lost her sister. She was doing what she had to do to find answers. He couldn't be mad about that.

Griffin ushered him out of the house as if he knew the struggle he'd been in. Wanting to see Noel before they left.

He offered to drive, and Griffin got in the back seat. He didn't question it, but found it odd.

"You okay, Duke?"

He looked at Griffin through the rearview mirror. "Yeah."

"Because if you weren't, I'd get it. The day Eve left me to confront her brother, it was one of the hardest things I had to do. Stand back and let her handle the problem herself. I almost caved. It's not easy standing back. So I understand if you're not okay. I sense Noel means something to you."

Duke had no idea what she meant to him. It was supposed to be casual. Just sex. Every day it seemed to be turning into something he quite couldn't put his finger on.

"I'm sorry I don't agree with how you two handled it this morning with Warren. She should've never gone in there alone. But I'm okay."

He wasn't ready to share his feelings about Noel, especially since he didn't know what they were.

Nick entered the vehicle, which dropped the conversion. "Let's go."

Since it was Tuesday, Duke knew they'd find Gregory at the soup kitchen and not at home. He parked in the back of the lot so Gregory wouldn't notice his truck right off the bat.

Duke pulled out his phone. "Tell me your number. I'll text you so you have mine. Call if you need backup."

"Okay, partner," Nick drawled, doing as Duke asked, then exited the vehicle.

Damn, that man could be such an asshole. Of course, it hadn't started this bad until he learned he'd slept with his sister.

Duke would not regret what he'd done with her. Their time together was nobody's business but theirs.

"He's protective of her. I wouldn't take it personal."

Duke didn't even bother looking at Griffin through the rearview mirror. Because he *was* taking it personally. That guy hated him. And why? He wasn't a bad catch. He didn't hurt Noel. He shouldn't be the bad guy.

14

NOEL APPRECIATED Eve helping to distract her by insisting she bake some cookies with her. When Nick told her they were leaving to interview Gregory, she wanted to go with. One stern look and shake of his head told her it wouldn't be happening. It was one thing to let her talk with an eighty-year-old guy who wobbled on his feet at times, it was another to let her interview someone who could've been the man who attacked her.

She understood. It didn't mean she liked it.

Eve had already been in the process of baking when they returned from Warren's, so Noel jumped in to help. They were done before the men returned. She felt weird hanging in Eve's home when she could be in the comfort of her own. Well, her temporary home.

When she told Eve she was leaving, she insisted on coming with her.

"You shouldn't be alone. I know." Eve winced though with a smile hiding in it. "You don't want people hovering over you. I get it. But it's because we care."

"You don't even know me that well."

"Maybe, but this is my chance to get to know you. And I might look small and weak, but two people are always better than one in a dangerous situation."

"You don't look small and weak." She knew Eve had defended herself against her brother. Standing up to a bully would never make a person look small and weak to her.

"We'll bring some cookies with."

Noel wouldn't argue with that. They were simple sugar cookies, cut out into Christmas shapes, of course, but they were delicious. Melt in your mouth delicious.

"Okay, you twisted my arm."

It was silly to move from one place to the next when they could've done the same thing in Eve's house, but she felt better in her domain. Eve had sensed that, which was why she didn't argue with her.

They munched on a few cookies. At least four for her. They were too good not to devour. Then she popped some popcorn and channel surfed until she found a comedy on TV. She ate some of the popcorn, but not a whole lot since she'd stuffed her face with too many cookies.

The movie helped to lift her mood and take her mind off what Nick and Griffin were up to. Duke as well.

They'd been in the same house and he hadn't sought her out. He didn't say hi.

What did it mean?

Did it even matter?

She would be leaving town, and what they had had been casual. Nothing more. She never went beyond casual. Duke wasn't an exception; he was the norm. Because after her childhood, she knew happily ever afters didn't exist. Not for people like her. With tons of baggage.

A knock on the door startled her, then she chuckled. "I'll get it."

She couldn't believe she let a knock surprise her. Looking through the peephole first, she was surprised to see Juliet on her doorstep. She opened the door.

"I heard about what happened to you. I wanted to check on you, make sure you're okay."

Wow.

That was kind of her. She didn't know her well either, yet she went out of her way to check on her.

"I'm fine. I'm feeling much better." She waved Juliet in.

"Hey, girl," Juliet said in greeting to Eve, taking a seat next to her.

Noel resumed her seat, noticing it was a bit more crowded with three people on the couch, though she didn't mind. It was nice to have company. And with two women who felt like they were becoming friends.

She leaned forward, frowning. "Shouldn't both of you be at work? At the cafe?" It was the middle of the afternoon.

"It's my day off since I worked the weekend with the festivities," Eve said. "Though the cookies I made are for the cafe tomorrow. You got to try them first."

She felt even luckier for that.

"I own it, so I can leave whenever I want, and I wanted to check on you." Juliet grinned, popping her hand into the popcorn bowl Eve held on her lap.

Juliet made a good point. Being the owner would give her certain luxuries.

"Did Griffin tell you what happened? Or Duke?" Either was plausible.

Juliet chuckled. "Oh, you're so cute, city girl. The whole town knows what happened because that's how small towns operate."

Oh. Well. That was disconcerting.

Which meant the whole town knew she had dinner at Duke's. Alone.

"And what are they saying about it?"

"They have no idea why someone would want to hurt you. Most think it was a mugging. I don't think anyone has any idea it's because Beth was your half-sister." Juliet's expression softened. "That piece of information was given to me by Griffin. I'm sorry for your loss."

Tears were rising. She could feel them wanting to break free, and she didn't want them to escape. But hearing condolences was foreign. No one had given any when they first found out about Beth, because of course, they hadn't told anyone. Not even her boss. She told him she needed time off and she'd call when she was ready to come back. No doubt, by now, she didn't even have a job anymore. She hadn't bothered to call him back, and he hadn't reached out either.

"I wish I could share some insights about Beth. About her time here. She never let anyone in. I tried, especially because she worked for me. I'm sorry to say I was pissed when I thought she left town. Left me high and dry. Then Eve came into town, saving me, saving the cafe being down an employee, and I pushed her out of my mind. God, I'm so sorry for that."

"It's not your fault, Juliet." She didn't want anyone to feel guilty. Beth was who she was. At times, Beth had been like that with her. "You gave her a job. You tried to be a friend along with an employer. There's nothing else you could've done. Let's talk about something else."

Because otherwise she would burst into tears, and she swore she was done with those.

"Totally. Let's talk about you and Duke."

Silence coated the room. If a pin dropped, it could've hit the floor and pinged softly.

Juliet giggled. "Yeah, I know. I don't know how to mind my business. I bet a hundred bucks Eve didn't pry once. She wouldn't. She's thoughtful like that. I guess I'm not."

That had Noel laughing with her. "There's nothing to talk about."

"Oh, but the town talks, remember? You had a fish fry with Duke. Alone. How did it go? Was the fish any good?"

As if Duke never made fish for her. The impression she got was he was very close with the Stuarts. That included Juliet, as she was a Stuart.

"The fish was delicious."

"That was a euphemism for something else, right?" Juliet gave her a devious grin.

Eve slapped Juliet's knee with a light tap. "Stop it. You're embarrassing her. What did or did not happen is not our business." Eve turned her head toward her. "Unless you wanted to share."

Oh, now Eve wanted to know what transpired between them.

"I mean, hypothetically, if anything happened, it was casual. Nothing serious."

Juliet licked her lips, her eyes begging for more. "I'm all for casual. I had the most insane sex with Lila's brother, Aster, and it was very liberating."

"Holy shit." Noel burst out laughing. "Does Lila know?"

"Umm, yeah. I'm sure the whole town knew. Small town, remember?" Juliet stuck out her tongue, a smile brimming beneath it. "Who says a woman can't have a fling when a man can without a problem? It's stupid how much we're frowned upon when we do something like that. After the marriage I had..." Juliet shivered as if remembering things she didn't want to. "I wanted something different for once.

To escape in a moment of pleasure. There's nothing wrong that."

Eve set her hand on Juliet's leg. "No, there's not."

"Okay, I had sex with Duke. In multiple places in his house. It was very satisfying, and I wouldn't say no to it again."

Juliet pumped her fist in the air while Eve giggled, holding her hand to her lips.

"That makes me happy." Juliet then winced. "He's kind of had a thing for me. I don't tell you that to make things weird here. Just telling the truth. I've always ignored it because he grew up with my brothers. He's like a brother to me, and I hated hurting him like that, not returning his affections. So to see him so happy, makes me so happy. You have really put a smile on his face."

Had she?

She liked the thought of that. Since what they had was casual, she would not let herself get jealous at the thought he'd pined for Juliet. Why wouldn't he? She was beautiful with her long brown hair and emerald-green eyes. Successful. Confident. Any man would want her.

"So, like what places in the house?" Juliet asked, her eyes brimming with anticipation to hear every sordid detail.

Noel wasn't about to go into detail. One, she didn't kiss and tell. Not even with her girl friends at home. Two, even if they never dated, they had a past together. It would be weird.

"Because sometimes, Aster and I would barely make it through the front door."

Okay. Mentioning a few of the spots wouldn't hurt. She wouldn't describe it all.

"I can confirm I know what that's like," she replied.

Eve slowly raised her hand. "Me, too."

Then they all burst into giggles.

DUKE GLANCED at his watch as Nick opened the truck door and got back inside. "You were in there for forty-five minutes."

"And all was good. I didn't call for backup, now did I?"

Griffin cleared his throat. "So what did he have to say?"

"Well, the first thirty minutes I was waiting for him. He hadn't arrived yet."

Duke groaned, rolling his eyes. "You could've told us that. Texted me. We were starting to worry about you."

"About moi?" Nick drawled, placing a hand on his chest. "You shouldn't have."

"And when he arrived," Griffin prodded, "what did he have to say?"

"Not much. He's a real asshole. Claimed Beth never approached him about it. I called him out on his bullshit, he told me to get the hell out before he threw me out."

Griffin drew himself back against the seat with a huff. "So it went as well as if we would've went in there and interviewed him."

"Yeah, but again, the difference between you and me," Nick said, looking at Griffin, "I'll find leverage to make him talk. Beth would've never just approached the grandfather, she would've talked to him too. Family was everything to her. She was always searching for more family. It makes me sad and a bit mad that Noel and I weren't enough for her."

"What do you mean by leverage?" Griffin asked, though warily as if he didn't want to know. And, Duke suspected, he wouldn't want to.

"Oh, I shouldn't say."

Duke chuckled under his breath as he started the vehicle. "I don't doubt it."

He parked in Griffin's driveway a short time later. When they walked into his house, they found it empty. But Griffin found a note on the counter from Eve they were in the cottage.

"I'll let her know we're back," Nick said in way of goodbye, leaving the house.

"Are you going to tell me what he meant by leverage?" Griffin asked before Duke could leave.

"I never told you how I got the footage of Beth and Warren arguing. You didn't pry further."

Griffin's brows puckered as if he didn't want to know the answer.

"Nick gave it to me."

"I suppose I don't want to know how he got it."

"No, I don't suppose we want to know that. All I know is he's good with computers. Draw conclusions from that."

"Great." Griffin ran a hand through his hair. "Well, tomorrow, head to Rosetta's and ask about the footage. So we have evidence the legal way."

Duke grinned. "Already done."

"Good man."

Duke said goodbye to Eve as he exited the house and she entered. He even waved to Juliet who got in her car that was parked on the street. He was glad to know Noel hadn't been alone while they were gone. He knew that Eve had been with her, but knowing Juliet had been as well was nice too. There was strength in numbers.

He waged another war with himself about visiting Noel before he left. He couldn't decide if he lost the war or won when he knocked on the door.

Nick hollered for him to enter, so he opened the door.

He sat on the couch with his computer on his lap. Noel was nowhere in sight.

"You didn't even know who it was. You should keep this door locked."

Nick rolled his eyes. "Dude, like you were going to leave without seeing my sister. Yeah, right. I knew it would be you."

Was he that predictable? He hadn't thought so.

"Keep the door open. I won't have any hanky-panky going on here."

This guy was asking for him to sucker-punch him.

"Find out anything yet?" Duke decided to ignore his threat, jerking his head toward the computer.

"Just started, but I will. Do you want to know if I do? It's not exactly...lawful what I'm doing."

And Duke believed in the law. In right and wrong. In following the rules. But hell. Since he'd met Noel, he'd broken a few of the rules already. Trouble, trouble, trouble.

"If he killed Beth...if he hurt Noel, then I don't care how you do it to get him to talk."

That was the honest truth.

At some point in time, the casualness of their relationship had turned into something more. Something he didn't want to put a name to quite yet. But that was as close as he'd get to it for now.

"Glad we're on the same page." Nick went back to fiercely typing on his computer, stopping for a second to add, "The door still remains open."

Duke chuckled, walking past him and toward the bedroom. The door was open, but he knocked on the frame before peeking inside. Noel rested on the bed with her back leaning against the wall and her legs stretched out and her feet crossed.

"Can I come in?"

She patted the open spot next to her. He slid his shoes off before sitting down. His thigh touched hers. His shoulder and arm as well. Even his toes grazed hers. He wanted to be as close to her as possible.

"Nick said it was a bust."

"Yeah, but he's working his magic right now."

She pressed her lips together, then twisted them with her nervousness peeking through. "You don't have an issue with...what he's doing."

"I'm pretending I don't know." Duke picked up her hand, linking fingers with her. Then his other hand brushed the faint bruise on her neck. "Gregory will pay if he did this to you."

"I hear you have a thing for Juliet."

Wow. Abrupt conversation change. His eyes rounded as his fingers went slack. If she hadn't increased the grip, he would've let her hand drop.

"She's not afraid to speak her mind. Don't worry. I'm not jealous. We're not exclusive."

Maybe he wanted them to be.

"Do you love her? She grazed the bare minimum of the topic, but I got the impression that you love her as more and she only loves you as a brother."

A week ago, knowing that would've killed him. Gutted him. Eviscerated his heart. While he mourned the loss of what could've been something great between them, it didn't hurt as bad. Not when another woman had taken a hold of his heart, like talons digging in, refusing to let go.

"I did. An infatuation that turned into love, or at least, what I thought was love. She started dating Gerald in high school. He was charming and loved by everyone in town. No one would've imagined she was living in the horror that she did. I didn't even see it, and I looked at her more closely than most people since I loved her.

"When she divorced, I thought she needed space. Time to heal. Then it turned into, I don't want to ruin our friendship. I don't want to risk ruining the friendship I had with Griffin and Bryce. Then another man waltzed into her life, and I realized I lost my chance. But I think the truth is I never pursued my chance because deep down I knew it would never happen. That she'd never see me as more. She deserves someone willing to take a chance. And I deserve someone that sees me as more."

Saying it out loud, really hearing it, made it drive home he'd done the right thing never announcing his affections. They were never meant to be. Because if they had been, they would've been together a long time ago.

Noel cupped his cheek, rubbing her thumb in place. He hadn't shaved this morning, forgetting to in all his worry about what to do about the woman currently touching him. Now he wished he would've so it didn't feel as rough. That if he kissed her, he wouldn't leave a burn behind.

"I have never been with someone so open and honest. Most men would've dodged that question."

"I don't want anything but honesty between us. Always. Even if the truth hurts. It's by far better than any lies."

"Do you hate me? For the lies?"

He closed his eyes, relishing in the way she still caressed his cheek. "How many times do I have to tell you I don't hate you?"

"I'm not good at this stuff, Duke."

His eyes opened.

"I don't understand anything other than hate. I grew up with it. I mean, with an abusive father, what could it be other than hate."

He moved closer, kissing her. Tenderly and with the utmost patience, even though he wanted to devour her lips. But now wasn't the time for that.

"What happened, happened. You didn't tell me everything right away. But now there's no lies between us, and let's keep it that way. I'm not mad. I don't hate you. And I want to kiss you so hard and so long until there's nothing between us but heat and skin. Then I want to sink deep inside you and lose myself into the pleasure that you always give me." His lips met hers again, giving her a small taste of he wanted. "But your brother is a short hallway away and told me to keep the door open. So I can't do any of that. Not without risking his wrath."

"You're being cock blocked."

"So painfully, yes." He groaned with laughter before kissing her one more time. A bit more passionately than the ones before.

"He can be such a pain in my ass."

"But he loves you. He cares about you."

Duke had a feeling he was also falling in love with her. A deeper and truer love than he had ever felt for Juliet.

15

"Hey!" She giggled when her brother turned his head, dazed and confused on why she'd slapped him on the back of the head. "I said your name like twenty times."

"Right. Yeah, I heard you."

She rolled her eyes, smirking, then caught Duke's eyes. Even he had a smile on his face at her brother's idiocy.

"We're hungry. I was thinking of ordering a pizza." More laughter came out as another round of eye rolls happened. "Yes, it's suppertime. You've been on the computer all afternoon in your own little world. You missed the hot sex session."

Nick set his computer to the side and stood up so fast Noel figured he wanted her to be afraid. She was never afraid of his posturing. "I know you're joking. You better be joking."

"I was totally joking. But not about you on the computer all day. Take a break. You know it gives you a headache when you stare at the screen so long."

"Fine. Go order the pizza." Nick glared at Duke. "You don't have to stay."

Duke grinned. "I don't mind. I like pizza."

"And what did you two do all afternoon?"

Noel thought about teasing him some more, but sometimes it was better not to tempt fate too much. She didn't know why he was in such an uproar about her and Duke. Her sex life wasn't any of his business. She didn't get involved in his. Every time he knocked on her door, looking for a place to crash because his wife kicked him out again, she let him in. She let him avoid whatever issue it was that time for her to get upset. He could damn well give her the same courtesy.

"Relaxed."

She had needed it. After the intense workout session they had this morning, her body was feeling it. The aches and pains from using muscles she hadn't in a while were protesting. At one point, she even thought about asking Duke for a back rub. She refrained because she knew it would've turned into more, with or without the door open.

Before her brother could interrogate her further with her one-worded answer, she started searching on her phone for a pizza place. Duke, knowing the town better, took over, ordering from what he said was the best joint in town.

She expected it to be shaped like a snowman or Santa or Rudolph or something when it arrived. Then she was disappointed when it wasn't. But Duke had been right. Best pizza she'd had in a while. Her brother and her picked different places all the time in the city, liking to change things up at times. Some places did it better than others.

With no alcohol in the cottage, they settled for water.

They hadn't done much grocery shopping, and she wished she had more to offer Duke. She tried not to let something so silly embarrass her.

"I hate to ask, but how is the search going?" Duke looked

relaxed in his chair, but Noel saw the tension in his shoulders. The slight ticking in his cheek.

He didn't like what her brother was doing. She couldn't say she was a fan either, but sometimes the situation called for it. Anything to find who killed their sister.

"So far, nothing. The dude is squeaky clean. His finances all seem in order. His social media is above board. He doesn't post radical or crazy shit. The soup kitchen doesn't seem to have any issues. He's not on any dating sites that I saw. The guy, though he's an asshole, isn't providing me any good leverage."

"I could—"

"No!" was delivered by not just one, but both macho men.

"I don't trust him," Duke added, that tick in his cheek increasing. "I wasn't happy about you visiting Warren either. You will stay away from Gregory."

Nick snorted, then coughed to cover up a laugh.

Yeah. Her brother knew she didn't take orders well. A lifetime of being told what to do had turned her into an adult who bucked at that whenever it happened. She'd lost a few jobs because her bosses had been a little more demanding than she appreciated.

But she understood why Duke wanted her to stay away. It didn't mean she liked it.

"I got Warren to talk." She unscrewed the cap from her bottle, taking a sip. "Just saying."

"I have to agree with Duke on this one. Hell no. The guy is a sleaze. I didn't like him one bit."

"Fine." She fiddled with the cap. "What do we do next?"

"We?" Duke straightened in his chair. "While I appreciate Nick trying to talk to Gregory today, there is no we here. *You* need to stay out of this investigation. What happened to leaving town?"

"*We* decided we weren't ready. Not until Beth's killer is caught." She made sure to emphasize the we because they were a team whether he liked it or not. He wouldn't have gotten a lead without them. "And we're close. I wouldn't have been attacked if we weren't."

Duke nearly reached for her hand across the table, but stopped. The look on her brother's face told her why.

"You getting attacked is why it's best you stay out of it. Why you should go home."

"You can sit there and tell me what to do and I don't have to listen to you. I can do whatever I want."

"I can arrest you for obstructing justice and tampering in an investigation," Duke retorted.

"Woah." Nick held up his hands. "Let's all calm down. There's no need for hostility here. You two spent the after-noon *relaxing* and now you're at each other's throats."

Her brother said it as if they'd made love all afternoon. Ha! They didn't do anything but talk. About random, stupid things. About the town a whole lot. Things that had happened in the past. Events he enjoyed the most. They didn't dig deep into anything personal about either one of them. It's as if they knew it was a topic off-limits. Once they ventured into that territory, it took whatever was between them from casual into serious. She wasn't ready for that.

Duke stood up. "I think it's time I leave. Nick's right. We need to calm down, and I don't want to say something I'll regret. I will do anything to keep you safe, Noel. That includes locking you up if I have to."

He left, the door closing with barely an audible click.

"I'm afraid that man might be falling for you."

Noel shook her head. No. What they had was temporary. A meeting of bodies. Nothing more.

"I won't stop him from arresting your ass if you don't stand down." Nick rested his elbows on the table. "I don't want to see you get hurt again. I can still see the bruise on your neck. I don't like seeing that."

Geez! These two were acting like she was going to jump right into danger. Wave a red flag and say, "Here I am" to the killer, "Come get me."

"I didn't say I was going to do anything. I asked a simple question, 'What are we doing next,' and he jumped down my throat."

"Yeah," Nick said with a heavy breath, "because that's what happens when a person is scared for someone they care about. I'm not sure staying is the right move here." He held up his hand. "And if we do stay, you should keep your distance from Duke."

Or what?

That's what she wanted to snap. What was he going to do about it?

"You're right."

Because nothing good would come from getting closer to him.

DUKE FIGURED if Gregory wouldn't give them straight answers, the people around him would. Provided they weren't scared of him.

He did his normal routine in the morning, checking out the murder board, staring for a long time at the new lead. Beth arguing with Warren. Then he left the house for work, stopping to grab his coffee. As usual. He was supposed to have the day off. Three full days since he worked so many doubles over the weekend, but he had too much to do on this case. He wasn't going to sit around waiting for something else bad to happen.

He popped into the precinct to make sure he wasn't needed for anything else, then off to the soup kitchen he went.

During the whole time, he was damn proud of himself for not dwelling on Noel. Because he'd had a hard time sleeping thinking about her. Thinking about the way he left the cottage. The anger between them.

Over something so ridiculous. Her safety was important. Why couldn't she understand he was trying to protect her? Keep her from harm.

He interviewed all the people in the building. Even the individuals who came for assistance. They saw Gregory all the time. They knew what kind of person he was.

Except nobody could corroborate that he'd ever spoken to Beth there. So if she had confronted him, it hadn't been at the soup kitchen.

He'd worked all morning and into the afternoon talking to people. Which meant he had to grab a late lunch. The meal he ordered at the cafe was delicious, as always. He had another few hours on his shift, and then he could clock out.

Then his mind would no doubt wander toward Noel and what she'd been up to all day.

"You bastard."

Duke turned around on the sidewalk, having just exited the cafe and heading to his patrol car. Gregory stood there, his fists clenched. The man would be stupid if he threw a punch.

"How can I help you, Gregory?" He wasn't even going to acknowledge the insult.

"You don't believe me—oh because I know Nick questioned me for you—that I never spoke to Beth about being my half-cousin. So you decide to harass my employees. The people who come in looking for help. How dare you!"

"I'm doing my job. I'm sorry if you see that as harassment."

"Why not take my word for it?"

Duke crossed his arms. "Oh, I don't know. Maybe because you have an insane idea that your brother is an innocent man and that right there tells me you have a hard time with the truth."

"For the last time, since you didn't have the balls to question me yourself, I did not know what Beth was talking to my grandfather about. She never approached me about the issue. She never told me anything. Not once. Not even when I saw her in the cafe. My grandfather never reached out to me about it either. Hell, when I went into the cafe, Beth acted like a damn mouse. Didn't like getting near me. Always had Theresa help me. So I rarely even talked to her then. Believe me. Don't believe me. I don't give a shit. But stay away from my work or I'll file harassment charges against you."

With that, Gregory spun on his heels and stormed away.

Duke pondered everything he said. Then walked back into the cafe.

"Hey, Theresa. Got a minute?"

She stopped wiping down a table and flashed him a pretty smile. "Of course. What's up?"

"When Beth worked here, did she ever help Gregory? Did they ever talk longer than normal? Or whisper with each other?"

She had to have confronted Gregory somewhere.

Her ponytail fluttered behind her as she shook her head.

"Oh, no. I don't recall them ever talking much. She always found a reason or another not to help him. I don't blame her." Theresa winced. "I don't know why he comes in here anyway after what his brother did to Juliet. Acting like everything is fine. I said some mean things about him to Beth. Told her to watch herself around him. That whole family is trouble. He can pretend all he wants like he's some do-gooder running the soup kitchen, but that whole family is evil."

Duke couldn't disagree there.

"Why do you ask?"

He smiled, hoping to hide the real reason. So far, only him and Griffin and the Benson's knew Beth was related to that family. He hoped to keep it that way—for now.

"Just following up on some stuff. You know me, I won't stop working her case until it's solved. Did she ever mention going to Bathington or Rosetta's a lot?"

Another shake of her head. "We didn't talk a whole lot. I mean, don't get me wrong, I tried. But she always kind of blew me off." She snapped her fingers. "It was so random I never thought about it before. She was dressed up all pretty and I joked if she had a date. For a brief second she got a wistful smile on her face and then gave me an abrupt no. But you mentioning Rosetta's, that being such a nice place, I bet she did have a date and didn't want to tell me. She was dressed way too nice for anything else."

"Thanks, Theresa. Do you remember when this was?"

Theresa bit her bottom lip, her brows scrunching together in concentration. "Maybe three weeks before she disappeared."

A date. A possible lead. Though he didn't know where to begin to expand on it other than visiting Rosetta's.

So he did.

Being in his uniform told Rebecca manning the hostess stand that he was there on official business. She got Roger, the manager, very quickly.

"I didn't think I would see you back here again. I gave you the footage you asked for. Without a warrant," Roger stressed.

Duke was very grateful about that. He didn't think him returning would be such an ordeal. While it was early afternoon, he suspected Roger didn't like the appearance of law enforcement on the property. Bad for business. He had gotten lucky he didn't need a warrant, considering he didn't have jurisdiction in this town.

"This won't take long." Duke pulled out the still photo of Beth at the bar. "I want to find who killed her. I know I asked before if she ever saw anyone else here. But I have new information that she was here on a date. About two weeks before this incident happened." Duke tapped the photo.

Not accurate, but he had to get Roger to talk somehow. Bluffing worked at times.

"How would I know that? I don't keep tabs on every single person that comes into the restaurant. I didn't even know the incident, as you call it, occurred."

"One of your waitresses knew about it." Which was how Nick and Noel knew to search the security cameras.

"Yeah, well, Stacy likes to get into everybody's business."

Perfect.

"Is Stacy here?"

Roger groaned. "Give me a moment."

Stacy appeared before him a few minutes later. "Roger said you have questions about Beth. Something about a date."

"Yes. I know two other people were here asking about Beth." He didn't mention they were Beth's siblings in case they never mentioned that information. "That you told them about the argument between her and an older gentleman, which I did see on the security cameras. About two weeks before that happened, I have reason to believe she was on a date. Possibly here."

Stacy shook her head, very animated. "I would've told them that too. She never met anyone here. Ever. Always came alone. The only time someone approached her was the older guy."

"Hmm. Must've been somewhere else she went then. Or she dressed up all the time coming here?"

"Well, yeah, most people do. But she didn't doll herself up or anything as if she were meeting someone."

"Thank you for your time. If you remember anything else. Anything that even seems insignificant, I'd love to know." Duke handed her his card.

"Sure thing."

Duke stopped at the bar. Considering Beth sat at the bar a lot, it wouldn't hurt to question the bartenders. Two were working. Lucian and Todd.

"I won't keep you gentlemen long. Just a few questions about Beth Terden. You heard about her death, right?"

Both men nodded.

"Terrible what happened to her," Todd said.

"How can we help?" Lucian asked.

"Stacy seems like she has a keen eye, but I wanted to ask you two as well since she sat at the bar a lot. People get to talking and all that."

Both grinned as if they knew what he meant. Bartenders acted like therapists at times. Listening to people's woes.

"Was she dating anyone?"

Todd laughed. "I have no idea. Lucian helped her more than I did."

"Not that I was aware of. She didn't mention any guy to me." Lucian tossed a thumb toward Todd. "He's right. I usually helped. We chatted, but about inconsequential things. She always had a sad look in her eyes. I didn't pry. I would try to make her laugh or something. But she never talked about herself, what might've been bothering her."

"No one, besides this gentleman," Duke held up the still photo to show them a picture of Warren, "ever bothered her?"

"Nope. Only him. I thought I was going to have to kick him out." Lucian gritted his teeth. "Real asshole to her. She was near tears by the time he left."

"When was the last time she came in?" It wasn't a question he had asked Roger or Stacy. That was an error on his part.

Though he knew she had worked the morning shift at the cafe the day before she disappeared. She had been seen in the drug store buying a few essentials, though after how many months, Bonnie couldn't remember what she'd purchased. And Beth had used cash, so no credit card receipt to verify. Once she left there, no one could account for where she went next. She never showed up to work the next day. By the second day of being a no-show, Juliet had called her brother to do a wellness check when Beth wouldn't answer her phone. They had found her place cleared of her belongings, her car gone, and had assumed she left town without telling anyone.

They had still yet to find her car. They had swept the lake, looking for it or anything else that could've provided a clue. It hadn't been dumped there.

Todd blew out a long breath, thinking. "I don't remember, man. Sorry. I mean, she came in like once a week.

Sometimes twice a week. I don't remember if she came in again before she disappeared."

Lucian scratched his head. "I think that argument with the old guy was the last time I saw her. I don't recall seeing her after that. I do remember wondering why she didn't come in again."

"Okay, thank you for your time. If you gentlemen remember anything else helpful, call me." Duke handed them his card.

That still put the drug store as the last place anyone had seen her.

What had she done that evening? Had she gone anywhere? Who had she seen?

Who the hell killed Beth Terden?

16

"I'll be back."

"Hold up!" Nick rose from the couch leisurely, but she knew he'd be ready to jump ten feet in the air to stop her from leaving. "Where do you think you're going?"

"Besides sparring this morning at the gym, we've been cooped up in this cottage all day. I need to get some fresh air."

She needed to see Duke. The way they parted yesterday bothered her. While she didn't have the guts to reach out to him today, he apparently didn't feel the need to either.

So one of them had to make the first move? To apologize. Nothing more.

"I'll get some fresh air with you."

"It's fine. I'll be fine."

"You're not leaving this house without me."

Huffing, she crossed her arms. "I was going to go to Duke's. Okay? I don't want you there."

Nick groaned. "I thought we decided it was best to stay away from him. I'm sorry I worked all day on the computer.

You're right. We've been cooped up too long in here. Let's go grab a drink."

"But I don't want to grab a drink. I want to see Duke."

"And what? What's the point?"

"To apologize or some shit. We didn't part on nice terms."

"Or some shit is what has me worried."

"What I do or don't do with a guy is none of your business."

Nick rounded the coffee table and grabbed her shoulders. "I don't want to see you get hurt. So I'm making it my business."

"Why do you have such a problem with him? You didn't before..." Before he knew they slept together.

He dropped his hands, laughing mercifully. "When have I ever liked any guy you've dated?"

Fair point.

Duke made his shit list the moment he ventured into the dating category. Not that they were dating.

"Sometimes, I need to help steer you away from trouble. So let's leave, get fresh air, get a drink. Come home."

Trouble.

Yeah, she knew Duke would be trouble. Her brother wasn't wrong.

"Fine. Buy me a drink."

When they arrived at Frost's Pub and Grill, the place wasn't as busy as it had been on a Friday. No surprise there. It was a Wednesday. They grabbed seats at a table instead of the bar. Nick ordered them two drinks at the bar while she stayed at the table.

She met Anton's gaze. The slight twinkle in his eyes told her he was happy to see her again. Weird.

Or not.

This was the first time she'd ventured into the bar since having dinner at Duke's. Alone. While they had gone to the festivities, they'd kept to themselves, keeping an eye out for Warren, the old guy they had tried to identify. They hadn't interacted with many people. This was the first chance for people to acknowledge the rumor running around town that she had a thing going on with Duke. Anton wanted to know more, and he couldn't ask questions if she wasn't at the bar.

Good thing her brother picked a table. She didn't want to talk about her and Duke.

"We could play pool. I could kick your ass."

She took a sip of wine, chuckling. "You wish you could. I'd hate to make you cry."

"You know I school you at pool all the time. Why lie to yourself?"

It would pass the time. She appreciated her brother trying to cheer her up.

"Yeah, okay. You're on. Twenty bucks say I beat you in the first game in less than ten minutes."

It took seven. And she was twenty dollars richer.

Anton walked up to them with two new drinks, even though they hadn't ordered any, or even finished their first ones. "I thought you might need to refuel so you can keep kicking his ass. Impressive."

"I have many talents," Noel said, taking the drink. Her brother would drink less if she planned to have a little fun.

"I have a break right now. Twenty says I can beat you in five minutes."

She laughed, pointing her finger at him. "You are a naughty, naughty man. You're trying to con me. I don't know how well you play. It's not a fair deal because you've seen my skills."

"That's a good point. I'll play your brother first. Kick his ass, then the bet is on."

Nick stood on the other side of the pool table, holding onto the pool stick as if not bothered by anything. Or getting ready to use the device as a weapon. It was hard to read him until he spoke. "Are you flirting with my damn sister? In front of me?"

Anton chuckled, grabbing his own stick and adding chalk to the end of it. "Absolutely not. I'd never mess with Duke's woman. Bro code and all that."

Duke's woman?

Had Duke said that? Or was that how the town saw her? Or maybe just Anton?

"Well, it seems like you're flirting," Nick reiterated.

"Does it?"

"I'd have to agree."

They all turned toward the new voice. Duke himself.

Anton set the pool stick back down and moved away from the table with his hands up. "Nope. Not a chance. But you can't hurt a guy for being friendly looking out for his friends." He passed by her, then clapped Duke on the shoulder. "Be careful. She knows how to play." Then he headed back to the bar.

Noel wasn't positive if Anton was warning him about pool or her in general.

"Looking out for his friends?" Nick gripped the stick harder. "What does that even mean? We were minding our own business."

She scoffed, racking up the balls. "You're so dense, Nick. He was sizing me up. Seeing if I'm good enough for Duke here. The whole town thinks we slept together because of one little dinner together. Alone."

Nick huffed a short laugh. "You did."

Noel swore the few people in the bar went quiet for a moment, then resumed talking in the next.

"Well, now they do know. Thanks, asshole."

Nick chuckled some more. "Oh, gosh. I don't know if I hate small towns or love them."

"They grow on you," Duke's quiet voice answered.

Noel forgot he was standing there, hearing the whole embarrassing conversation. She couldn't quite tell by his stoic look what he was thinking about it all.

"Am I playing or is he?" Nick asked, looking back and forth at him.

"I suppose that's up to Duke."

"Sure. I'll play a round." He took off his jacket and tossed it on the back of a high chair. Anton delivered him a beer and walked away without one word. "Do you want to break? Or me?"

No, she didn't want to break. At least, her mind took his simple question and made it into something more.

She didn't want either one of them to break. She was afraid they were on their way to something of the sort if the tension between them continued. It circulated around them. Suffocated her. Reminding her of how it felt to not be able to breathe. Not being able to suck in a short burst of air.

"You can break."

Because she imagined he could heal his wounds, his heart, way faster than she'd ever be able to.

There was a reason she kept things carefree with men. Why she didn't open herself up to others and let them in. Because she couldn't break. She couldn't be forced back into her childhood where her father broke her every single day.

Duke walked toward her, needing to get by to get his own pool stick. He slowed, his hand reaching out as if he wanted to touch her. Yet it never made contact.

Then he passed her and grabbed a stick. The balls scattered everywhere after he hit the white ball into the triangle of balls. The sudden sound, even though she knew it had been coming, made her jump.

Duke noticed the jerk, hesitating, as if he wanted to say something, but instead, continued his turn after knocking in a solid.

She watched in fascination as he got in all the solids but one.

"Holy shit. I bet you're glad you didn't make a bet with him, Noel."

Well, if she had, it would've been more fun to make a bet that had nothing to do with money.

But fun always ended and sometimes even led to pain. And pain was never anything she wanted to endure. Not if she could help it.

"Game's not over, Nick."

Then she lined up her first shot, glancing at Duke out of the corner of her eye. His expression was unreadable. The way he remained quiet since entering the bar was unnerving. Why was he here? Had he known they were here?

Why wasn't he saying much?

Here she thought she wanted to see him, and now when she got her wish, she didn't know what the hell to say. Thank goodness he wasn't talking.

It was time to wrap up this game and leave.

❄

DUKE HATED the awkwardness between them. They'd had their share of misunderstandings and issues since she arrived in town, but never this kind of doomed tension.

He'd worked hard all day trying to find more answers in Beth's case and then went home, hoping he could relax and not think about Noel. Except all he did was think of her. She was imprinted everywhere in his house.

As soon as he walked in the front door, images of taking her hard and fast pelted his brain. It happened again in the living room, and then in the kitchen. He couldn't escape her no matter how much he wanted to.

Did he want to?

The way they left things burned a hole in his heart. So he got in his car expecting to knock on her cottage door, but saw their rental car in the parking lot of Frost's. Now that she was in front of him, he had no idea where to start. What to say. It didn't help that her brother was in the vicinity either, or the other patrons in the bar.

If it hadn't been known before, everyone knew the truth now. They'd slept together. Thanks to Nick blurting out what he had.

Duke couldn't find an ounce to care that anyone knew. He wasn't embarrassed or ashamed. He had no reason to be. What they had shared had been beautiful, pleasurable, and nothing he regretted.

He watched in awe as she proceeded to do the same thing he had done. Pocket every ball. But the difference was she managed to get all the stripes in, then knock the eight ball in the side pocket. She even called the shot.

Game over.

"Nice job."

The smirk that she wore turned him on. Though, to be fair, it didn't take much to turn him on when it came to her.

"Thanks."

Stilted, awkward conversation. How did they get past this?

"I didn't gain a whole lot of ground on your sister's case today."

Nick perked up at the news, as if surprised he decided to share that. Noel gripped her pool stick so hard he could see her knuckles were turning white.

He wasn't sure why he decided to bring up Beth's case, but he knew it was the right call. He'd told Noel to stay out of it, and that was what started this tension between them in the first place. That was the last thing he wanted between them.

"What did you find out?" Nick asked. "Anything at all?"

Duke waved them closer, not wanting to share all the details with the entire bar. If one person in here heard, the whole town would know. Not that rumors weren't swirling around already by the questions he asked. It would get out sooner rather than later. They ventured closer, congregating in the corner.

"No. I decided to try a different tactic with Gregory and interview the people around him to see what they might have witnessed. No one saw Beth confront him about anything." He leaned on his pool stick for support, needing it a bit. Noel was listening but not looking at him. "I'm starting to believe him that she never told him they were cousins. Someone would've saw something if she had."

"I don't know. It seems odd she wouldn't tell him, but told his grandfather," Nick replied.

"It does. You're right, until you look at more of the facts. She worked at the cafe. Juliet was married to his brother, who was very abusive. While Juliet doesn't talk about it a whole lot,

Theresa wasn't shy about it. She warned Beth about him. Would that make her keep her distance from the guy? Because I'm thinking that's why she never approached Gregory."

Nick mulled that over. "It does make sense. Warren's older. A frail old guy, for the most part. She wouldn't have felt threatened with him. But Gregory is a tough looking guy when he gets angry. You could be right. He could be telling the truth. I still haven't been able to find any dirt on him. The guy has an attitude problem, but he's pretty clean otherwise."

Good to know, not that he liked knowing how Nick was obtaining that information.

"Where does that leave us..." Nick grinned. "You, in your investigation. I mean, if Gregory didn't know anything, why would he kill her?"

"I'm not sure. But I'm not quitting. I will find who did this."

Nick looked at Noel, then at him, rolling his eyes. "I'm going to use the bathroom."

Then they were alone. Duke knew Nick didn't like what was going on between him and his sister, but he was nice enough to give them a few minutes alone.

"I'm sorry I got upset yesterday."

Her gaze lifted. Finally! The sadness coated in her beautiful hazel eyes gutted him. "Me too. I'm not a fan of people telling me what to do."

"I'm not trying to tell you what to do. I..." His fingers brushed the bruise that was fading on her neck. "I don't want to see you get hurt. Again."

When his hand dropped to his side, Noel grabbed it, linking fingers with him. "Thank you for the update. I know you didn't want to."

"I shouldn't since it's an ongoing investigation, but I wouldn't be where I'm at without you two."

He rubbed his thumb over her soft skin, loving the way her eyes lit up with pleasure. Gone was the sadness.

"I had no idea you were such a pool shark."

A wicked smile spread across her face. "There's a lot you don't know about me."

"That's something I want to change."

She averted her gaze, biting her bottom lip. Even her hand slackened in his. Okay. So she wasn't on board with that idea. Good to know. He pushed her too far into a territory she didn't like. Casual it would remain between them.

"How about another game of pool?"

"Yeah, okay." She slipped her hand out of his and started racking up the balls.

He hated how she ignored what happened. The conversation she wanted to avoid. But he pushed the annoying emotion down and tried to put on a smile. If moments like this were all he was going to get, he'd take it.

Nick returned, his eyes narrowing as he looked back and forth between them. The tension was still there. This time more visible, thicker and suffocating. Nick could feel it too, yet he didn't ask why they didn't make up while he'd given them the space to do so.

They were on the verge of making things right between them when he opened his dumb mouth and tried to expand on their relationship. At least he knew where he stood with her.

"Why don't you play this time, Nick?" Noel didn't give him much of a choice. She put her pool stick back and sat down at a table.

"Sure." Nick broke the balls, missing getting any in the pockets. "I know we came to the conclusion Gregory isn't lying, but could he be threatening people to stay quiet? To lie about anything they might've saw."

Duke thought about it as he lined up his sights at the striped ten ball and took his shot. Missed.

That proved how affected he'd been by Noel's rejection. Though she hadn't actually said a word, she had rejected him and anything that could've moved their relationship to something deeper. Perhaps even more permanent. Eve's relationship with Griffin, and even Lila getting together with Bryce told Duke that distance didn't matter in the long run. He wasn't going to worry about the fact she lived how many states away in a big city.

Duke backed away from the table to let Nick have a shot. "I don't think he threatened anyone. They didn't seem scared or anything when I interviewed them. Like I said, Theresa was a wealth of information about Beth and how she warned her about Gregory."

Nick took a shot. Missed. "What else did Theresa talk about?"

Duke eyed the table, wondering what ball to try for next. "It didn't pan out. She thought maybe Beth had a date or something a few weeks before she disappeared. Mentioned how she dressed up one day. I did go back to Rosetta's and check it out, but Stacy said the only person to ever show up was Warren. Beth never met anyone else."

He lined up a shot and missed again. Damn it.

"Did she always dress up going to Rosetta's?" Nick asked.

"According to Stacy, for the most part, but she didn't *doll herself up* is how she put it. So maybe Theresa saw her on a day that she intended to go to Rosetta's when she normally didn't give that kind of thing away. It's probably nothing."

Nick circled the table before taking another shot. Missed.

Noel groaned. "You two need to up your game. This is ridiculous. Focus!"

They were playing like shit, especially when he'd looked like a pro the first game with her.

"I'm done." Noel stood up, putting on her jacket. "I've had enough fresh air."

Nick set his pool stick down, offering him an apologetic grin. "We'll finish this game another time."

Duke doubted that.

One minute they were there, and the next they were gone. It felt the same way they'd parted yesterday.

Anger and tension swirling in the air.

Duke grabbed his beer and took a seat at the bar.

"Well, that didn't go well," Anton said leaning his elbows on the bar.

"I messed up."

"Or you didn't try hard enough."

Duke looked at Anton, who was smiling at him like a Cheshire Cat.

"Some people waltz into our lives and it's not a big deal when they walk back out. And then some people, you shouldn't turn your back on. Noel is one of those people. Hell,"—Anton straightened, his low chuckle renting the air —"a woman who can play pool like that is a woman worth pursuing. That was hot as hell what she did."

It had been pretty damn impressive.

Duke pointed a finger at him. "No getting hot and bothered by her. No more flirting either."

Anton held up his hands in surrender. "You got it." Then his wicked grin widened. "Don't think I'm stupid either. We both know the first time wasn't at your house." He winked. "So don't be an idiot and let her get away. Someone like her only comes along once."

Well, shit.

He wasn't wrong.

But he'd tested the waters a little bit ago, suggesting he wanted to know more about her, and she'd fled. She told him loud and clear she didn't feel the same.

So where did he go from here?

He'd never been in this kind of situation before. He had no idea how to proceed.

17

NICK LEFT her alone the entire ride home. He let her get ready for bed without one word. She even got comfy under her covers before he strolled into the bedroom, sitting on the edge of the bed.

"We need to talk."

Her back was to him, her eyes trained on the wall. If he insisted on dredging up what happened, then he could do it with her back to him. Why did he care anyway? He didn't like the thought of them together.

"Noel..."

"Talk, then get out. I want to go to sleep."

"What happened at the bar with Duke? You were hell-bent to see him and then there he is in front of you and you flee like a scaredy cat. What the hell? What happened when I went to the bathroom?"

Not that much happened. They apologized to each other.

Then he offered her an olive branch.

A way to stay tethered together. To get to know each

other a little better. To keep what was happening between them alive.

"I don't know. I don't want to talk about it."

"Did he say something that hurt you?" Nick gripped her shoulder, as if ready to roll her to his side.

"No. He was a gentleman the entire time."

"Then what happened?"

Maybe it was the sad sigh he released, but she found herself flopping her body the other way. Nick let his hand drift away from her.

"Nothing. I swear. He...he scares me."

Nick frowned, anger swooping in.

"Not like that, you idiot." She closed her eyes. "He makes me want things I've never wanted."

"Hey," he whispered, waiting until she reopened her eyes. "It's okay to put your heart out there for once. I know I've been a dick about you two, but not because I think Duke's a bad guy. He's really not. In fact, he's the kind of guy I would never worry about you dating. If he lived closer. I was being a jerk because I didn't want what's happening right now—you to get hurt."

"I'm not hurt. He didn't hurt me."

"You're sad, which indicates you're hurt. I think it's time we leave, Noel. My boss has been pretty lenient about my absence, but he's not going to be for much longer. Your boss..." Nick laughed. "You need to look for a new job."

Yeah, she knew her job had gone to shit before they even left. Nick wasn't wrong. It could be another few months before Beth's case had a break in it. Or years. Or maybe even never. It was a real possibility they might never know who killed her.

"I'm sure your wife misses you too."

"Doubtful." Nick ran a hand through his hair, sighing.

"When I knocked on your door to crash on your couch, I knew it would be until I could find my own place. I served her divorce papers."

Noel sat up, clutching his arm. "I'm so sorry, Nick. Why didn't you tell me?"

"Don't be. She was cheating on me. Had been for a while. I should've never married her. I got caught up in the whirlwind and I thought she was the one. I learned my lesson to be a lot more careful the next time. I was too embarrassed to admit it." He placed his hand over hers still holding onto him. "I never looked at her the way Duke looks at you. As much as it pains me, that man has it bad for you."

Noel was beginning to suspect as much. The way he'd said he wanted to get to know her more had frightened her. She didn't let guys get to know her. She didn't know how to dive into that kind of relationship.

"I don't know how to navigate something like that. It scares me too much."

"I know. It's okay, though, Noel. As much as it sucks it didn't work out between me and Steph, at least I tried. I attempted to let someone in. And maybe we didn't work out in the long run because I didn't give her my full self. Yeah, she cheated on me, but I had my faults in the relationship too. You can't always keep people at a distance. Beth did too. Hell, she even kept us at a distance. We all three grew up with a shitty childhood, and it's made us create barriers. At some point, we need to let those barriers go. You have to let someone knock it down."

Let Duke knock it down.

"I was a bitch tonight to him, leaving the way I did."

Nick laughed, patting her hand and letting his drop. "Yeah, you've also lied to him and he didn't seem to be turned away from that. Tomorrow is a new day. We'll do our sparring and then you can talk to Duke. Settle things between you two. Then I think it's time we leave."

She let her hand fall away from his arm. "You're confusing me. It's like you're saying put my heart on display with him, but also let him know I'm leaving."

"Well, we can't stay here forever. And if he wants to see you again, he can come visit us. Long-distance relationships are a thing."

She'd never even had a close-distance relationship. How would she manage a long one?

"Hey, sleep on it. You don't have to make any major decisions now. I don't even know why the hell I'm encouraging you about this."

She didn't either.

"But maybe I want to see you happy for once."

"I'm happy."

He gave her a tired grin. "You're content. But you're not happy. I'm not even happy. That's why I know my marriage was a mistake. Even then I wasn't happy. And maybe we're both destined to live unhappy lives. Who knows."

She shoved him. "Now you're depressing me."

"I'm depressing myself." But he leaned in, hugging her. She held on, not letting him go right away. They didn't show affection much. Not in this sense. Because they didn't get it a whole lot growing up. But deep down, she knew her brother loved her as much as she loved him. They showed it in different ways.

He pulled away, squeezing her arms in affection. "I think, despite everything that has happened, this trip was a good idea. We've learned a few things about Beth we never knew, got a bit of closure, and we learned some things about ourselves."

Good points.

"It is kind of funny. Our mom was a lover of Christmas to the point she named us after the holiday and managed to get our birthdays close to the stupid holiday. And part of Beth's family is from a Christmas town. What are the odds? It's so ridiculous, it's funny."

"In a way, it makes me feel closer to her. More connected. I like that we shared something silly like that with her."

"Me too." Nick leaned forward and kissed her forehead. "Get some sleep. Try not to worry about anything. It'll all look better in the morning. It always does."

She doubted that.

Nick left her room, leaving the door open. The light from the hallway turned off a few seconds later. It didn't mean he was going to sleep as well. He'd mess around on his computer because he loved being on the device. It was his passion more than anything else.

She fell asleep. Her dreams started peaceful and light-hearted. Her and Duke having fun at the lake. Memories of their times together, laughing and having fun. Nothing negative touched her mind.

Then in a blink of an eye, they turned dark and evil. A faceless man in the corner, waiting to attack. She tried to get away, but he caught her, jumping on her from behind. His hands wrapped around her neck, shoving her face into the ground.

He squeezed.

And squeezed.

The air in her lungs couldn't escape. A tiny breath was out of reach. She wanted one small breath to leave. To let her know she could survive.

She wasn't ready to die.

"Noel!"

She felt herself being jerked in her sleep, but her body felt lethargic. Her lungs clogged, unable to catch her breath. Like in the nightmare she was having.

"You have to get up." Nick coughed. "Come on. Get up."

Her senses took a few moments to adjust. The room was dark—and smoky.

Nick coughed some more, trying to cover his mouth as he did. "We have to get out of here. We have to climb out the window." More coughing attacked him.

She found herself joining him in the onslaught of coughing, crawling out of bed as she did. Smoke was everywhere, it was difficult to see. But it didn't take a genius to know why. There was a fire somewhere. In the background, she even heard the fire alarm going off. Why didn't she hear that sooner? Before the smoke enveloped them in a massive cloud of white.

Nick shoved the window open, hitting the screen until it popped out. "Come on, you first."

He helped her up and through the window. She didn't land gracefully, falling on her right arm hard. She screamed at the pain. Then Nick was jumping down next to her a lot more agile than she'd landed.

"Come on, we have to get away from the house." Nick pulled on her to get up, but her eyes blurred, a bout of dizziness attacking her.

Maybe she inhaled too much smoke. But she didn't feel right.

Another coughing attack hit her, to the point she couldn't even move. So Nick did what he always did. Protected her. He grabbed her and threw her over his shoulder, getting as far away from the house as he could.

They barely made it past the side of the house before it exploded, throwing them both through the air.

She didn't remember anything after that.

DUKE GROANED, rolling to his side, picking up his phone. It was two thirty in the morning. Why was someone banging on his door? He got out of bed, rubbing his eyes, then grabbed a pair of sweats and a shirt before heading for the front door.

Griffin stood on his porch, the expression in his eyes one of dread. Duke's heart pounded, not wanting to hear whatever he had to say.

"Is Eve okay? What's going on?"

Because Griffin didn't show up at his house in the middle of the night. If it were work related, he would've gotten a phone call. For him to show up like this meant something bad had happened.

"Eve's fine. I don't know how to say this, so I'll just say it. Nick and Noel are on their way to the hospital."

He had to grip the door for support. Not just Noel, but Nick too. That meant something very, very bad happened.

"There was a fire at the cottage. They managed to get out before the gas tank in the back of the house exploded, causing the cottage to go up in flames. It knocked them pretty far though. I'll drive you there."

He swallowed hard. Words were incapable of releasing. Duke found a pair of shoes by the door, not even bothering to grab socks. Then he grabbed his keys, locking the door with shaky hands, and followed Griffin to his car.

His best friend even used the sirens to get them there faster. By the time they got to the hospital, his nerves were so wired with fear, he thought he was going to throw up. Griffin informed the nurse in the emergency room who they were and why they were there. Then they were directed to a set of chairs to wait for news.

He was in a daze about it all. This couldn't be happening. He saw both of them a few hours ago. They were fine. They weren't laughing and having fun together, but they were fine. They left fine.

Bryce appeared, taking the seat next to him. It made him wonder how much time had passed for him to arrive.

"The fire department got the fire contained. It didn't hit any of the other houses," Bryce said in way of greeting. Or maybe he had said hello and Duke didn't process it. "Is he okay?"

"He'll be fine," Griffin answered, as if it were true.

But was he okay?

He didn't think so. Noel was hurt. Again. And why? How had this happened?

That question pulled him out of his daze. "How did the fire start?"

"Someone started it. I don't know who," Griffin answered. "I heard the explosion, and it jolted me out of bed. I found Nick and Noel on the grass between our houses, the house in flames. Nick was awake, but stunned. Noel was unconscious. I'm pretty sure they inhaled a lot of smoke before getting out, by the way Nick was coughing so much."

"And Noel? She woke up before the ambulance arrived?" Because Duke knew it had to have taken a bit before they arrived. They had a fire department in town, but not a hospital. The fire crew would've seen to their injuries before an ambulance could.

"No, she didn't."

That wasn't a good sign. Considering she'd been

knocked out a few days ago, a second knock to the head would be bad. Fatal, even.

"She's in good hands here, Duke. You know that," Bryce said as if his words would be a comfort. He wasn't wrong. Lila had received care here when she'd been attacked with an axe. That had been a scary time as well. But head injuries weren't anything to mess with.

"Did you check the cameras you have outside the house?"

Because after the incident with Eve and someone breaking into the cottage when she first moved to town, Griffin had set up cameras around the outside perimeter. Since he owned the property, he had a right to do so.

"I checked the cameras while we waited for an ambulance. No one approached the front. The back door was a different story. I couldn't see the guy's face. It was too dark and he wore a hat, shielding his face. There was a logo of some kind on the hat, but I didn't recognize it. I asked Nick if he heard anything, and he said he didn't hear a sound. He woke up surrounded by smoke and flames. He barely heard the fire alarm going off in the background. He said he ran to Noel's room and had to shake her awake."

"Someone started the fire. Near the gas tank." Because the oven and dryer worked off gas. Eventually, it would've caused it to explode. Killing them instantly if the smoke hadn't done it first.

"It appears that way," Griffin answered.

"Why?" Duke shoved his hands through his hair. "They stopped looking into Beth's case. I know they did. I've been handling it. Why not go after me?"

"Yeah, but you didn't start looking into anything until after they told you what they found. This person didn't like that."

"Which means I'm close to the truth. They were close to the truth."

"Bring me up to speed," Bryce said. "Another set of eyes on the case can't hurt."

So Duke and Griffin did, explaining the visits with Warren and Gregory, the few pieces of information he'd gotten from Theresa, and how the visit at Rosetta's proved fruitless. Before Bryce could offer an opinion, a nurse interrupted them.

"The gentleman, Nick Lancaster, has seen the doctor and can be discharged. You're welcome to go speak to him."

Duke shot up out of his chair. "Which room?"

She rattled off a number and the three of them went together. Nick didn't look surprised to see him. If anything, he looked relieved.

"They told me Noel's still not awake." Nick's eyes filled with tears. "I didn't get her away from the house fast enough. I didn't—"

Duke moved closer, setting a soft hand on his shoulder. "You got her out though. You did your best, Nick. Stop blaming yourself."

"I inhaled a bit of smoke, a few cuts and bruises from the explosion, but otherwise I'm fine. While my sister isn't waking up. If she wouldn't have hit her head a few days ago..." Nick's face morphed into fury. "It was same guy who did this. It has to be."

Griffin stepped closer to the bed on his other side. "We agree. I wished the security cameras gave us a better clue to who this guy was."

"So the first time this guy strikes," Bryce piped in, "what did you two do that day?"

"Nothing much. We didn't even leave the cottage until Noel went to get some food for us. I was on my computer all day..." Nick glanced back and forth between him and Griffin. Oh, he knew he'd been trying to hack into Rosetta's system. "The day before we were at the parade and the festivities keeping an eye out for Warren, who we didn't know his name at the time. We went to Bathington as well, showed his picture around. No one recognized him. I guess I know why now. The dude's a recluse. We went to Rosetta's again, asking more questions about Beth."

Bryce pointed at Duke. "Yesterday you went to Rosetta's too, asking questions, didn't you? That, right now, is the common denominator before both attacks happened."

Bryce had a point, but he didn't know what stood out as the issue. What was he missing?

"The manager couldn't remember anything from that timeframe. Stacy did, but she didn't tell me anything useful. Neither did the bartenders. I don't know what I'm missing. Theresa thinks she had a date one time, but no one at Rosetta's can corroborate that."

Nick adjusted his position on the bed, coughing as he did. "Maybe she didn't have a date. Maybe she was dressing up nicely for someone already there. Stacy mentioned to us that Lucian, the bartender, had a sweet spot for her. The guy himself even admitted to asking her out, but Beth said no, that the time wasn't right."

Holy. Shit.

"He told me she looked sad a lot of the times she came in, would try to make her laugh. He never mentioned he asked her out."

Fury erupted on Nick's face. "Now why would he tell us, but not you?"

Duke could think of one reason. Because he was a cop.

"I hate to say it," Bryce popped in, "but the fire could've been his way to fix his little mishap. Maybe he didn't mean to tell Nick and Noel that he asked her out. So he had to get rid of the only people who knew."

Duke would make him pay if this turned out to be true.

"I asked him the last time he saw her, and it was the same day she argued with Warren. I'll press him further about it. If he's lying, I'll get it out of him." Duke wouldn't settle for anything less. Not if he'd been the one to hurt Noel. "Right now, I sense he lied."

"Get me a computer. I'll find out if he's lying."

Duke looked at Griffin, who then looked at Bryce, so Duke looked at him as well. Neither man spoke up that it was a bad idea. And, oh, it was definitely a bad idea. It was very illegal, in fact.

Then Bryce took the decision out of his hands. "I have my laptop in my car. I'll be right back."

"He's not that smart if he thought he could get away with this." Griffin crossed his arms. "The fire chief will find out the fire was deliberately started. I have it on camera that it was. What was his end goal here?"

"To shut us up. Permanently." Nick shuddered, then had a coughing episode.

Lucian was going to regret ever laying a finger on Noel. Duke would make sure of it.

18

DUKE WAS ITCHING to go pick up Lucian and question him further. Now that the seed had been planted in his mind, he wasn't doubting they were on the right track. He could feel it in his gut.

Why the hell couldn't his gut have acted up when he interviewed the guy?

They'd moved to Noel's room where she lay so quietly and still in the bed. The doctors weren't worried—yet. Head trauma was a finicky thing. They were monitoring her vitals and brain activity and so far everything looked normal. She would wake up. Or so they said.

Not even Griffin or Bryce had left, sitting in the corner with him while Nick typed furiously away on the computer.

"Got in!"

Duke sat up straighter in his chair. He figured Nick had an easier time getting into Rosetta's security system because he'd done it before.

"So, this part could take a while. I have a lot of videos to go through."

He despised they were doing this illegally, but he also couldn't force himself to tell Nick to stop.

"Start with the last day she was seen. Her last known whereabouts was at the drug store in Sleighville in the early afternoon. Now, no one else could remember seeing her at Rosetta's. But it was a while ago. Their memory could be faulty."

They waited while Nick did more crazy tapping on the keyboard and then went silent, doing minor clicks here and there as if scrolling through the videos.

"That bastard."

Nick swiveled his computer around. There, in the parking lot of Rosetta's, Lucian was seen talking to Beth in her car. The timestamp at the bottom of the video said he saw her around nine o'clock that evening.

"Does he leave with her?" That asshole had lied to him. Liars only told stories for one reason: to cover up the truth.

Nick turned the computer back toward himself, silent again. "No, she leaves the parking lot." Then he was silent again. "But he does leave thirty minutes later. In a hurry."

"Did his shift end then, or he left early?" Griffin pondered out loud. "That's one of the things we'll need to find out. Maybe he left and met up with her and things went wrong. They didn't seem mad at each other in the video."

Duke stood up. "I'm going to go find out."

He did not care one bit it was four thirty in the morning.

"I'll go with you." Griffin stood up as well.

Nick looked at Noel in the bed. "I want to go with, but I don't think you'll let me, and I can't leave my sister."

"I'll stay with you," Bryce offered, flashing Nick his political smile. Though Duke knew he was being sincere.

"I told you I'd find your sister's killer. I will get the truth out of him."

Then Duke and Griffin left. He wasn't dressed for an official visit from law enforcement, so they stopped at his house first, then Griffin's so he could change as well. Eve wasn't home, and Duke wasn't surprised. He wouldn't want to be alone after what happened next door either. Eve had gone to Lila's house, which was how Bryce knew to come to the hospital.

Lucian didn't live in Bathington, he lived in Cannon, which was closer to Sleighville. If he and Beth had met up outside of Rosetta's nobody in either town would've known. But people in Cannon would've. Unless they never saw each other in public. He also didn't live in a community, but on a property surrounded by woods. What would he find if he took a look around?

Duke banged on the door until it swung open to a disheveled man who'd been woken out of a good sleep. Or at least, he wanted them to think that.

"Hi, Lucian. Remember me? Officer Fisk. This is Chief Stuart," Duke said, motioning to Griffin next to him. "We have some more questions about Beth Terden. Can we come inside?"

"The sun isn't even up. Why so damn early?"

"Well, there's been a development in the case. Someone saw you speaking to Beth the night she disappeared."

Panic filtered into his eyes.

Oh, he had him dead to rights.

"Do you want to explain why you lied to me about when you last saw her?"

"It was a long time ago. I don't remember every time I saw her."

"You were sweet on her. You liked her. You asked her out. She declined," Griffin stated.

The panic rose in his eyes. But he wasn't dumb. No

admittance filtered out. "I was friendly with her. I told Officer Fisk she was always sad looking. I tried to cheer her up."

"And you asked her out? Did she not take the rejection well?"

"I don't know what you're talking about."

Okay. He wanted to keep lying to him. Fine.

"So that last night, was she sad? Did you want to cheer her up then too?" Duke probed. He wasn't leaving this house without a confession.

"I...can't remember what you're talking about. She was sad most times she came into Rosetta's."

"A simple warrant will get me further access to Rosetta's security system. I will find you speaking to her in the parking lot that night."

They both knew it was true. But he didn't add he'd already seen the evidence. Plus, Lucian thought there was a witness that saw them talking.

"Did you work a full shit that night?" Griffin asked. "Or leave early? And I would answer truthfully because cameras don't lie."

"Do I need a lawyer here?"

"Do you want a lawyer?" Duke asked casually. "We're just asking questions. We haven't arrested you." Yet.

"I can't remember if I left early that night or not. Rosetta's closes at eleven. I usually stay my entire shift."

Yet, the security camera told a different story. That he had left early. About an hour early. He could use the long timeframe as an excuse not to remember something like that. It wouldn't get him very far. Not with evidence to back up the truth.

Griffin shifted his stance, glancing behind Lucian, though Duke wasn't sure what he was looking at.

"Where were you this evening?" Griffin asked. "Around two in the morning, to be exact?"

Okay, so they were shifting gears. Because all they had was him on camera talking to Beth. He didn't leave with her. Sure, he lied about when he last saw her, but that wasn't a crime, per se. The amount of time that passed could be plausible that he didn't remember the last time he saw her. They had nothing to prove he killed her unless he confessed. And confessing to Nick and Noel that he had asked out Beth didn't say he killed her either. But it helped build a case against him. Especially since she had declined his invitation. Maybe he didn't like getting rejected. Maybe she rejected him again that last night and he followed her in a rage.

"Sleeping. Where else would I be?"

"Setting fire to my cottage that I rented to the two people who were related to Beth," Griffin answered. Although he had a short grin on his face, his voice held a cold, calm violence to it.

"You two have lost your mind. First you think I had something to do with Beth disappearing and now I started a fire? Get off my property, especially if you're not going to arrest me."

Griffin pulled out his handcuffs. "Well, you are under arrest for arson and attempted murder. Put your hands behind your back."

"With what proof?" Lucian spat back.

Griffin pointed behind him. "I got you on camera. And I told you, cameras don't lie."

Lucian must've realized he was pinned in a corner, because he turned and tried to run. He didn't even make it halfway through his living room before Duke tackled him to the ground. He even threw an extra punch when Lucian started to struggle with getting cuffed.

Then he hauled him to his feet, jerking on his arms when he still struggled. "We'll add resisting arrest to that list."

Griffin gestured toward the hat lying on a side table. "Interesting logo on the hat." It had a circle with a DM in the middle. It stood for some company or organization. Duke had never seen it before though. Griffin leaned down to sniff it. "You spilled some gasoline on it too. Sloppy. Very sloppy."

As Duke walked him to the patrol vehicle, Lucian had stopped struggling. The man knew he'd been caught.

He got him inside and closed the door before he lost his control and beat the living shit out of him for hurting Noel. And Beth. They'd prove it sooner or later.

"I'll call in the cavalry. You solved your first murder, Duke."

Yeah, but not on his own. He'd had help.

But he didn't care how it happened.

All he wanted was for Noel to be okay and wake up. Even if it meant she'd walk out of his life. The case was solved. There was no more need for her to be in town.

NOEL WASN'T proud of her actions. Because when she woke up and noticed the sterile, bland surroundings, she freaked out. She went hysterical. If her brother hadn't been there to calm her down, she would've hurt a few of the nurses who only wanted to help her.

"Get me out of here. Now."

She didn't care what her injuries were or what the doctors said, she wanted out.

Nick didn't hesitate. While he left to get her discharged, Bryce stayed with her. A man she didn't even know. Someone she just met. "Can't say I blame you. I have nightmares of this place. Lila wasn't here that long ago and...and I didn't like seeing her like that. But you hit your head hard—again. You should stay for a bit."

"I know you're trying to be kind, but nothing you say will get me to stay here."

Her head killed her. Pounded like those nails had been driven back into her skull and never left the first time. Her arm, that she had landed on jumping out the window, was sore, but not broken since it wasn't in a cast or anything. Her whole body was sore. They'd flown through the air by the force of the explosion. They were lucky to be alive. If Nick hadn't woken up and gotten her out of bed, they would've never made it out alive.

"What time is it?"

Bryce glanced at his watch. "Almost noon. You've been out a long time. Your brother was pretty scared. I was scared, and yeah, I know I don't know you. Doesn't matter. You scared us all."

Interpreted as she should stay in the hospital.

She closed her eyes so she couldn't see the pleading in his. Some time passed, she wasn't sure how long, when Nick came back in. "The doctor signed off on discharging you but was not happy about it."

"Noted. I'm ready. Let's go." She sat up and twisted her body. It protested the movement every step of the way.

"Umm...Bryce, would you mind giving us a ride to Duke's?"

She snapped her gaze at Nick's. "Duke's? Where is he?"

"Busy interrogating the guy who tried to kill us and who killed Beth. He said we could crash at his place for now."

When had her brother talked to him? Who tried to kill them? Killed Beth?

"Stop it. Don't worry about anything. We'll talk about all of it later."

"I know where Duke hides a spare key." Then Bryce led the way out of the room.

While she didn't need help walking, she let her brother feel useful and hold her around the waist as they made their way to the car.

Bryce drove them back to Sleighville and straight to Duke's house. She felt safe and secure—as usual—the moment she stepped over the threshold.

"Lila and I will come check on you later. Get some rest. But don't fall asleep. Not that kind of rest." Then Bryce was gone.

Right. No sleeping. Because she'd suffered a major concussion and going to sleep and never waking up could be a possibility.

"Why don't you go lie down?"

She looked around the room, moving her head too fast, wincing. "Where will you rest if I take the couch?"

The look he gave her should've made her laugh, but she didn't have it in her to do so. "I meant Duke's bed. He told me he only had one and for you to use it. I'll add he wasn't happy to hear you wanted to leave the hospital. I wasn't happy about it either. But I know you wouldn't have stayed unless they drugged you. So do us both a favor and don't argue with me about anything. Go lie down in his bed. I'll be right in there."

"Can I shower first?"

She felt grimy from everything. Crawling into Duke's bed smelling like smoke and dirt all over sounded gross.

"Don't fall. If you can manage that on your own, yes. Otherwise, no."

She'd force herself to remain standing.

And she did. Barely. Her entire body felt so drained and weak. Holding one hand to the wall had been necessary through the whole process. But she managed to wash all the grime off and wash her hair without losing her footing once. She dried herself off and then froze in front of the mirror.

She had no clothes.

Everything had been destroyed in the fire.

Well, if Duke didn't mind her using his bed, he wouldn't mind her wearing some of his clothes. She grabbed a shirt from his closet and put it on, then crawled into bed. The underwear issue couldn't be solved with his clothes.

Nick walked into the room and closed the curtains, which she was grateful for. She should've done that herself. The bright light had hurt her eyes—and head.

"Here's some water." He set a water bottle on the nightstand next to her. "And I'll make you a strawberry smoothie soon. The doctor gave me a list of foods to help with recovery. Berries were one of them. You're going to have to avoid coffee for a while."

That sucked. She liked her caffeine.

"How was the shower?"

"I feel better." But still like shit.

"I'm going to grab one myself. Will you be okay for a while? Don't fall asleep."

"I'll be fine."

Nick grabbed some clothes from Duke's closet as well and then left the room. She was jolted a few minutes later by Nick shaking her hard.

"I told you not to fall asleep, Noel!"

Had she? One second he was walking out of the room and now here he was. That's all she remembered.

"I'm sorry."

Nick crashed next to her on the bed, shaking his head. "I should've made you stay in the hospital."

"I'm fine. I will be fine. Tell me what's going on. Talk to me to keep me awake." Because her mind still wanted to shut off.

So Nick told her how he'd hacked into Rosetta's security system again. This time in front of an officer and the chief of police. Wow. Then he relayed what she assumed was a modified version of Duke and Griffin questioning Lucian and arresting him.

They'd obtained a warrant for Rosetta's security system, getting the evidence the legal way that he'd seen Beth the night before she disappeared. They obtained a warrant for his residence and property. They found Beth's car hidden in one of his sheds.

The cute bartender who had pretended to their faces he liked Beth had killed her.

Then tried to kill them for looking into the matter. For knowing his secret that he had asked her out.

"Has he confessed yet?"

Nick leaned his head against the wall. Duke didn't have a headboard. "Not yet. Not that Duke told me." He picked up her hand and squeezed. "But he did it. They got him. They got him for the fire too. Can't see his face on Griffin's security system but they identified his hat he wore. A local town's baseball team. It smelled like gasoline. The clothes in his hamper did too."

They had him on arson at least. Of course, she had no

idea how he'd talk his way out of having her car hidden in his shed. Unless he killed her, of course.

"Why do you think he killed her?"

Nick shrugged. "We might never know. What matters is he didn't get away with it."

"When did you call Duke?"

Nick turned his head toward her. "The moment I walked out of the room after you woke up. I knew he'd want to know you were okay. You scared us all, Noel. No more hitting your head on shit."

"Yes, sir."

Then they laughed together and went silent.

She didn't fall asleep, but she did lean her head on her brother's shoulder. "I guess you're going to say it's time to leave."

"And you'll counter with you still haven't settled anything with Duke. You should settle things with him. You'll regret it if you don't."

She regretted a lot of things in life. One of them being leaving the bar last night so abruptly and acting like she didn't want to be near him. Then nearly died a few hours later, never having told him how she felt.

So yeah, she didn't want to regret anything else ever again.

19

Duke opened and closed the front door quietly. The living room was empty, but he found Nick in the kitchen.

"Hey."

Nick jumped around, shoving a hand to his heart. "Dude, you scared the shit out of me."

Duke chuckled, enjoying the light sound. It was the first time he'd done so all day. Even yesterday he hadn't laughed about anything.

"How's Noel?"

"Good," Nick said, bobbing his head up and down. "Resting. Of course, I haven't let her fall asleep. I've been in the bedroom with her most of the day keeping her awake. I just left her now to grab us a snack. Bryce and Lila visited a bit too and brought some dinner. Eve was here as well. She's had plenty of company to help keep her awake. I think we're over the worst of it."

Considering it was after ten o'clock at night, it was a good sign she hadn't lost consciousness again since this morning.

"That's great to hear. I'm going to grab a shower."

"Do you want to say hi first?" A low chuckle left Nick's lips.

"I need to shower, Nick. I feel disgusting. Being by that... asshole all day. I don't want to get near her when I've been by him."

The muscle in Nick's cheeks flexed and unflexed. "Did he confess?"

"I wish he had. He's not talking. But we found her car, and inside the car, we found most of her belongings. We suspect anything not there, he burned. There was a barrel behind the house where he burned things. Forensics collected everything. We have enough for a case. He's not getting away with it, even without a confession."

"Thank you, Duke. For everything. I appreciate it."

He offered a half-grin. "Thank *you*, Nick. Because I wouldn't have gotten this far without you two."

Duke left the room, grabbed some clothes from the closet in his spare room, and took a shower. A very quick one because he was eager to see Noel.

When he peeked his head in the room, Nick was nowhere in sight. Noel was lying down on her side, her back to the doorway. She didn't turn as if she heard him. Had Nick warned her he'd come home? If so, was her back turned away a bad sign he not enter?

No way to find out unless he ventured forward, or found Nick and asked first. He went with the first option.

Instead of crawling in bed and spooning her to his body like he ached to do, he rounded the bed, surprising her. She scooted up into a sitting position. He sat on the edge of the bed.

"You were gone a long time. Everything okay?"

"Of course. We got the guy. We were collecting all the evidence we could. How are you feeling?"

"My head still hurts." She winced as if to convince him, but he knew it had to be killing her. By the accounts from Nick, they had flown too far in the air. He didn't have a chance to break her fall. They both hit the ground hard.

"I'm glad you're okay. When Griffin knocked on my door..." He reached out and grabbed her hand. "I've never been so scared in my life. The thought of losing you..."

Shit. He needed to stop that kind of talk. She didn't want to get that close with him. To make their relationship something more than casual.

"I'm really glad you're okay."

He knew he sounded like an idiot repeating himself, but he couldn't help it.

"Are you going to bed? We can share it. I'm not supposed to sleep much though. Nick will be in and out of here."

"If you want me to be in here with you, I can stay."

All day, he had wanted nothing more than to be by her side. Hold her tightly and never let go. But his job had to come first. He had to make sure the person who hurt her got what he deserved. That her sister got the justice she deserved.

"Please stay."

He walked around to the other side of the bed and sat down next to her, though stayed above the covers.

"Tell me everything you did. Talk to me. I don't even care what about. I am getting tired so anything to keep me awake."

He figured she was getting tired because she'd had an exhausting day from everything. Getting hurt, waking up, trying to stay awake when her mind wanted to shut off.

So he told her everything he did like she asked. Every detail from the moment he knocked on Lucian's door to the moment he left the precinct to come home.

She popped in with questions or observations.

By the time they finished it was past midnight. Nick hadn't come in to say good night, but he'd bet his life savings he'd gone to sleep on the couch. He had also been injured today. He had to be exhausted taking care of his sister while also hurting himself. He obviously trusted Duke to take over for the rest of the night.

"I'll set an alarm to wake you up every hour on the hour. I'm sure it's okay to rest your eyes for a bit."

Since her eyes looked droopy already, she wasn't going to argue. And she didn't. She fell asleep rather quickly. Duke lay next to her, aching to touch her, but refraining from doing so.

The alarm jolted him out of a good sleep every time it went off. A necessary evil. Noel woke up easily every time he nudged her shoulder.

Nick popped his head in the room around nine the next morning, right before the timer would've gone off again. "How's she doing?"

Duke had woken up an hour ago, unable to fall back asleep. He'd called Griffin, taking the day off. There had been no explanation needed why.

"Good. I think she's over the worst of it. How are you feeling?"

Nick tossed a lazy shoulder up, but he saw the pain in his eyes as if he was hurting all over too. "I'm fine. I'll live. I thought I'd get us breakfast. I usually make her a hearty breakfast, but she does have to adhere to a certain diet while recovering. I thought I'd see if the cafe has something good. Want anything?"

"Whatever you want to grab for me is good. You can use my truck."

"Good, because I was going to anyway. Our rental was ruined in the explosion."

Duke chuckled as Nick disappeared from the doorway. He heard the front door close a short time later. He switched off the alarm and then brushed her shoulder with a soft caress.

"Hey, sweetheart, it's time to wake up."

"Hmm," she mumbled. "Already?"

"Yes, already. Talk to me for a few minutes and maybe I'll let you go back to sleep."

Her eyes opened slowly. They both lay on their sides, about a foot apart on the bed. Sleeping next to her all night without holding her had been one of the hardest things he'd ever done. But she'd made it plain and clear that night in the bar, they were done. No more getting closer to each other.

"Nick went to get breakfast."

"He's going to have me eating the grossest shit. I guarantee it."

"Because he's worried about you. He wants you to get better as fast as you can. I do too."

"My head doesn't pound anymore. A dull ache, like an annoying headache. Not like it was earlier."

"That's great. See, you're already on the mend."

She eyed him up and down, frowning. "Did you sleep above the covers all night?"

And have temptation at his fingertips? Hell yes he did.

"I was comfortable." He rolled over to the edge of the bed and got up. "I'll get you some more water and some pain medication."

"Okay. Thanks. I'm going to use the bathroom."

That was a good idea. He used the half bathroom he had near the kitchen first, even brushed his teeth with a spare toothbrush from under the sink. Because one never knew what could happen, especially when in close quarters with Noel.

He drank a glass of water himself, then grabbed her a glass and filled it to the top.

When he turned the corner, Noel had exited the bathroom. He couldn't tear his eyes away. This woman could drop him to his knees.

She stood with only his shirt on, reaching just past her butt. Did she have anything on underneath? The picture before him was pure temptation.

"You're so damn beautiful you make me weak in the knees."

"I used your toothbrush. I hope that was okay."

He nodded. She could use whatever the hell she wanted if she kept looking at him like he was the only man who mattered.

He closed the distance, holding out the glass and dropping two pills in her hand. She swallowed them and drained most of the glass.

"Your brother should be home soon." And climbing back into bed was a bad idea. Not that anything could happen. She had a head injury she was recovering from. "I should take a shower."

She fiddled her fingers against his. "Lay with me."

He couldn't deny her. Not in the innocent way she asked. He followed her into the room like a puppet on a string. She crawled under the covers, and he was right behind her. This time, being under the covers too, he was unable to hold himself back. He pulled her gently into his embrace, cocooning her in his arms. She wrapped her legs around his, as if needing to entangle them further so he couldn't escape.

He brushed his hand up and down her back, causing the shirt to move. When his hand brushed bare skin where underwear should've been, he froze. His hand wanted to move lower. Caress her ass, pull her closer to him.

So he did.

He gripped her bare ass, kneading it, before grinding his cock into her and pushing her ass to meet him at the same time.

She moaned, kissing him.

If she didn't have a damn concussion, he knew he would've been seconds from shoving deep inside of her.

IT HAD TAKEN every ounce of bravery she had to invite him back into his own bed. She knew he had wanted to flee, making an excuse to take a shower. His eyes had shown her he had wanted something different. The way they'd glazed over with desire, begging her to come closer.

She solved the problem for both of them. Because she wanted him just as badly.

Despite the feverous kiss between them and the way he grinded against her, palming her bare ass, she knew she wasn't up for more. Her head still ached.

Duke knew that too because he slowed the kiss, stopping it altogether, then halted the movements down below as well. Though his hard cock was still pressed firmly in the right place.

"God, I want you, Noel. You have no idea how badly. But not right now. Not like this."

She rested her hand on his chest, looking at that instead of his face. "I know. I did mean just lay with me. I'm sorry I tempted you."

His chest rumbled with laughter. "I don't think you're sorry."

Her gaze lifted to his, a tiny smile emerging. "You're right. Not that sorry. At least, not about that." This would be the even harder part. Where she needed her courage to shine through. "I am sorry about the way I left last night. Or two nights ago. The last few days have blended together."

"It's in the past. Let's—"

"No, Duke, let me finish. It's not okay. You put yourself out there, indicating you...wanted more, and I acted like an idiot. I'm sorry."

"Hey, we knew what this was going into it. Nothing more than...sex."

Had she read him wrong at the bar? She didn't think she had.

"My brother says long-distance relationships happen all the time."

Duke's brows puckered together.

"I can't say I do well with close-distance relationships either. In fact, I don't do them. Letting someone in, like truly in, is not something I do. It's not something I know how to do. We jumped into this thing without thinking, and I went along with it because I enjoy being with you. You were more than just having some fun."

"Noel..."

She winced, hating how he said her name. Full of regret. "Am I reading this entire situation wrong?"

His hold on her tightened when she flinched like she was going to try and move away. "No, you're not reading anything wrong. I have a lot I want to say, and I don't want to freak you out. I don't want to scare you away."

"We said nothing but honesty between us, even if it's hard to hear."

"Yeah, we did, but I don't want..." He bent his head closer, touching her forehead to his. "I don't want to lose you. My words could freak you out and you turn away from me. You were more than just having some fun for me too."

"Tell me anyway."

Now she needed to hear what he had to say.

"Okay. It might've started casual between us, but that ship sailed when you got hurt that first time. Hell, that night you left my house, you took my heart with you and I hadn't realized it yet. When Griffin knocked on my door and told me you were on the way to the hospital, the only thing I could think was..." His eyes closed. Tears glistened in the corner of his eyes when he reopened them. "The only thing I could think was I didn't tell you that I fell in love with you. That I didn't want to lose you. That I wanted to make this thing between us real. That we figure out how to do that together."

"I would love to figure that out with you too." She kissed him hard, so he would know she meant it. Or maybe she just needed another kiss. Because when their lips met, his grip on her ass strengthened, pushing her into his cock. "I'm pretty sure I'm falling in love with you too. It scares the hell out of me."

"Then we're in the same boat," he whispered. "Because I thought I was in love before, and now I know that was a fantasy I carved out for myself to protect myself. What I feel for you is different. It scares the ever-loving shit out of me."

"So what do we do now?"

The last time she'd asked him that question—though it pertained to a different matter—he'd gotten upset with her and left angry.

He blew out a slow breath. "If you were feeling better, I'd love you from head to toe to show you how much I love you.

Since you're not, I'm going to hold you. For a very long time, until you tell me to stop. From there, I don't know."

"I like the sound of that plan."

That's what they did. They held each other and must've fallen asleep because when her surroundings came into focus, there wasn't as much light peeking through the curtains as before and her head didn't ache any longer. Not even a dull one.

"Hey, sleepyhead," Duke whispered, kissing her. A quick brush of his lips. "I like watching you sleep. You make the cutest faces."

"I do not."

He grinned like the devil. "Oh, you so do."

"What time is it?"

"Midafternoon. I don't know. I let you sleep without disturbing you for once. I think you needed it."

"I do feel much better than this morning." Her lips twisted with unease. "Nick went to get me breakfast."

"And your brother understood. He popped his head in a few times."

"I should get up and tell him I'm sorry and thanks for the thought."

"You could if he were here. He left about an hour ago with Bryce. They went to buy you both new clothes and whatnot. He needed a new computer too."

"Oh, he's going to be gone forever. Buying a new computer is going to take him forever. He'll need just the right one."

"So I have more time with you all to myself."

"Yes, you do."

Duke brushed a soft hand down her back, cupping her ass. "Do you still want a shower?"

"It might help wake me up."

"Do you want company? In case you lose your balance or something, I can hold you up."

"Oh, for my safety, is that it?" she asked as she caressed his lips with hers.

"Yes, for safety reasons."

"Then you better join me."

Duke scrambled out of bed, but waited patiently while she took her time. He grabbed a new set of clothes and an extra T-shirt. "For you, when we get done. I find I like seeing you in one of my T-shirts. It's the most erotic, beautiful thing I've ever seen."

"And when my brother gets back? What then?"

"We'll hide in the bedroom again." Duke's naughty smirk had her loving that plan.

The hot water was soothing on her body, warming the aches and pains everywhere. Duke even massaged a few places—non-sexually—to help release some of her tension. They washed each other, lathering soap and taking their time to clean each other. When they stepped out of the shower, dripping wet, she saw the desire blazing as strongly in his eyes as it was in hers.

He dried her off, taking care when he touched her everywhere. She did the same, even though she knew he wasn't hurting in places like she was.

Then the towels drifted to the floor. She planted her hands on his chest. "I need you, Duke. I can't take it."

"I don't want to hurt you." But he grabbed her hand and guided her back to the bedroom, shutting the door and locking it for extra measure. Who knew when her brother would be back.

Then she settled into the middle of the bed while he put a condom on. He positioned himself above her, his face in turmoil.

"That shower was a bad idea. This is a bad idea."

She guided his cock to where it belonged and lifted her hips. "If it gets to be too much, I'll let you know."

He shoved inside the rest of the way, holding himself still, brushing her cheek. Then he pulled out and thrusted in, with an aching patience she'd never had before.

That's how it went the entire time. Slow, even thrusts that didn't jar her body or her head. Nothing rough between them. Only sweet, tender loving.

She gripped his arms, panic settling in her chest. "I don't think I can leave you. I don't think I can go back to New York."

He thrusted inside, stilling his movements. "Nobody said you had to. Because I don't want to let you leave. If it wasn't clear before, Noel, I love you. You belong with me. This house, everywhere I look, I see you. You surround me everywhere I go. At the bar. At the lake. Here."

She giggled, remembering their little adventures at each place. "I wonder how many other places we could have sex."

"You naughty..." He laughed, kissing her instead of finishing his sentence, continuing his slow, beautiful pace. "You don't have to go."

"I love you too." Her nails dug into his arms after she said it, as if a hole would appear and swallow her whole and only he could keep her anchored to the surface.

"We're in this together."

The crescendo hit soon after, with her moaning his name in the darkness. He stiffened, whispering more words of love in her ear.

Then a loud banging startled her. "This door should be wide open you two! Open it up before I pick the damn lock!"

They both laughed.

"Your brother isn't going to kill me for getting you to stay here, is he?"

"No, Nick isn't violent. But he can be devious. Don't hurt me and you'll be fine."

"You're safe with me. Always."

She knew that without a doubt. From the first moment she'd been wrapped in his arms, she had felt safe and secure. That should've told her then that he was the one.

EPILOGUE

Three months later...

"Woah, woah, woah! I'm losing my grip." The couch slipped from his hands, nearly hitting his left foot. Nick looked up to see Bryce laughing on his end. "Dude, not funny. I almost lost some of my toes."

"You should've saw your face. Priceless."

"Pick up your end and let's get this over with."

Noel had moved to Sleighville. Actually, she never even left. Nick went home to New York, packed her shit up for her and had a moving truck bring it to her. He hadn't had the heart to take her away from Duke's side. It was as if she needed him by her to feel safe. Nick couldn't explain it or understand it, but he didn't argue with it. For the first time that he could remember, his sister was truly happy. He couldn't find fault in that.

Before he left three months ago, he'd spent a lot of time around Bryce. The dude, for being a politician—even if it was a small-town one—was a pretty cool guy. They got along well. They even texted a lot when he left town. Bryce kept him up-to-date how his sister was doing on the off chance she wouldn't tell him herself.

Even Duke had.

She was doing great. She healed well, and the moment she'd felt better, Duke took over as her sparring partner. Nick laughed thinking about how that went. Because if she could kick his ass, that meant she could kick Duke's ass. At least, he hoped so.

She'd gotten a job at Frost's Pub and Grill. Whenever he talked to her, she had nothing but nice things to say about Anton. Between her and Lila, they wanted to find him a nice woman. Poor guy had no idea what was in store for him.

Two and a half months ago, after finalizing his divorce that went pretty well, he decided the city felt lonely. He needed to be by his sister.

Now, here he was, after settling all his affairs in the city, moving into a small house that he was renting. The same house Beth had before she'd had her life ripped away by that asshole. And he was still not talking. Not giving them a reason why he killed her. He hated that. Not knowing. Wondering what must've happened that night to snuff out such sweet innocence.

It made him feel better to know that he wouldn't be getting out anytime soon. If they couldn't get a conviction for her murder, at least he'd go down for the fire that nearly killed him and Noel. They had plenty of evidence to tie him to that. Of course, they had pretty solid evidence to tie him to Beth's death as well. It was damn hard to explain why her car and belongings were on his property.

They got the couch situated in the middle of the room and plopped down on it together. It had been the last piece to be moved inside.

"Thanks, dude." Nick sighed, needing a beer.

"Anytime."

His sister and Duke strolled into the room. "Last box is in your bedroom," Noel said. "You're all moved in. Welcome to Sleighville."

Bryce slapped him on the shoulder. "There's a box by the front door with Christmas lights. I'll help you hang those tomorrow."

"It's February."

"And you live in a town that celebrates the holiday year-round. The Christmas lights are going up," Duke replied, wrapping an arm around Noel.

Since he'd arrived in town, whenever he was around his sister and Duke, they couldn't keep their hands off each other. As much as he hated witnessing the lovey-dovey affection, he loved the happiness on his sister's face, so he never commented on it. Well, maybe he gagged a few times in jest.

"The tourists love that shit." Noel's face beamed with too much joy. "My shift starts soon, so I have to go."

"Thanks for the help."

Then his sister and Duke left, hand in hand and grinning at each other like lovesick puppies.

"Want to celebrate your move with a drink at Frost's? I bet we can get a few on the house from Anton." Bryce stood up.

"You had me at celebrate, but I won't say no to free beer either."

They drove separately to the bar. Noel was arriving as they did. She served him his first drink, and of course, said that one was on her.

The second one, Anton said he got it.

So the night went on like that, people buying him drinks. He'd be finding a ride home tonight.

"I hear you suck at pool."

Nick turned his attention to Juliet standing next to him. "You heard wrong. I am amazing at pool."

"Care to wager on that?"

"I never pass a wager with a beautiful woman. Name your bet."

"Loser buys drinks."

Nick stood up, pumped. "Perfect. I've been getting free drinks all night long. I'm not about to start paying now."

"Big talker."

He set up the balls, offering Juliet to break first. He didn't mind the view as she bent and lined up her pool stick. Oh, no. He didn't mind the delicious view at all. A nice round ass made for his hands.

What were the odds Bryce's sister would give him a chance?

The question forgotten, he got down to business at kicking her ass at pool. Or, at least, tried to. She was a lot better than he thought she'd be, and he wasn't sure why he thought she'd be bad at it when she'd challenged him.

He was lining up a shot with the eight ball and pulling the stick back when it hit something. He straightened and turned around to apologize and came eye to eye with Gregory. Not a killer, but still an asshole.

"Do you mind? You're in the way."

Gregory cocked a brow. "Or maybe you should watch your back."

Was that a subtle threat?

"Keep walking, Gregory."

"Or what?"

Nick wasn't sure who threw the first punch, but he knew he got in the last one. Knocked the asshole straight on his ass.

When he caught Juliet's irate gaze, he answered his own

question from before. No, Bryce's sister would never give him a chance. Not when he acted like he did.

WANT TO KNOW HOW GRIFFIN AND EVE MET? CHECK OUT DASHING THROUGH THE FEAR!

FOR GRIFFIN & EVE'S STORY, CHECK OUT
DASHING THROUGH THE FEAR
A SLEIGHVILLE NOVEL, #1

Welcome to Sleighville...where you are sure to have a holly, jolly time.

Running is her only option. He made sure of that. Where better to run to than the last place he'd ever think to look for her. Sleighville. A small, quaint town that celebrates Christmas—every. Single. Day. Just the thought makes her want to puke, but she's out of options. Nothing prepared her for small-town camaraderie. Everyone knowing everyone and everything. Where she lives, where she works, and worst of all...they know something is off. That she's not who she claims to be.

Griffin isn't sure what to make of his new neighbor, but one thing he does know: he can't resist a puzzle. She's skittish, wary, and one of the most beautiful women he's ever met. It's not hard to fall for her, which is bad. He has no doubt she's hiding something—or hiding *from* something. If only she'd let him in, trust him with her secrets. No amount of Christmas cheer is going to sway her his way, but patience and time might. Problem is, he fears he doesn't have much time. She's one step away from running. No doubt not her first time, but he'll do whatever it takes to make sure she stays right where she is. In his town, and in his arms.

For Bryce & Lila's story, check out
Here Comes Chaos
A Sleighville Novel, #2

Welcome to Sleighville...where mayhem meets murder.

Mayor Bryce Stuart's quaint Christmas town is in crisis. With holiday cheer fading faster than melting snow, he turns to a PR firm for a total holiday makeover. Amidst the tinsel-draped chaos and unexpected divorce papers, Bryce is determined to save his town even as his personal life unravels.

Lila Hansley, a PR whiz, would rather dodge snowflakes than deck the halls. When her grinch of a boss tasks her with reviving a town where yuletide seems cursed, she finds herself tangled in more than just stubborn locals and tacky decorations. Between Bryce's infectious Christmas spirit and his soon-to-be ex-wife's icy interference, Lila's job becomes a real-life holiday mayhem.

But when mischief escalates to murder, Sleighville's revival takes a sinister turn. As tensions rise and secrets surface, Bryce and Lila must navigate a web of small-town intrigue where someone's silent night just became permanent.

Can they uncover the mystery before their Christmas miracle becomes another holiday homicide? Or will Sleighville's dark secrets bury their efforts deeper than the winter snow?

ABOUT THE AUTHOR

I'm a *USA Today* Bestselling Author that loves to write contemporary romance and romantic suspense novels, although I am partial to romantic suspense. I even dabble in paranormal. Honestly, I love anything that has to do with romance. As long as there's a happy ending, I'm a happy camper. And insta-love...yes, please! I love baseball (Go Twins!) and creating awesome crafts. I graduated with a Bachelor's Degree in Criminal Justice, working in that field for several years before I became a stay-at-home mom. I have a few more amazing stories in the works. If you would like to learn more about me and my books, head to my website by scanning the QR code. Thanks for reading!

Scan me